CAPTAIN'S DUET

Destined
to
Dominate

Red Phoenix

Destined to Dominate: Captain's Duet
2nd Book of the Set

Cover by Shanoff Designs
Formatted by BB eBooks
Phoenix symbol by Nicole Delfs

Dedication

What a journey!

Writing Captain and Candy's story has been a joy and a crazy adventure. To write this story on both ends of the country and finish it in a new house with no furniture is something I will never forget.

MrRed took over the move from CA to FL and all things house and meal related so that I could devote the time I needed for this story. He has been amazing support.

Captain and Candy's story means so much to me, and I have come to love them with the same intensity as Brie and Sir.

Huge thanks go to my incredible editor, Karen, who took on this project knowing how nuts it would get. She's had my back the entire way.

Thanks to Anthony for his vision. This beautiful love story came to be as a result of several discussions we had on how to expand the Submissive Training Center world. I owe him for setting me on a path that led me to knowing Captain in a whole new light.

I wanted to do Captain's battle scene justice and am seriously grateful to Top Griz, who took the scene I envisioned and made it come to life. His experience and expertise made all the difference to that pivotal moment in the story.

I'd like to thank my betas Becki W, Marilyn C, and Kathy O. They also had to work under the wire but were big supporters of the story.

I want to recognize my kids, Jon and Jessica. You continue to amaze me with your dedication and creativity in marketing my books. Having my children, who know me so well and believe in the stories I tell, means so freaking much to me. I am so honored to be your mama!

My special thanks go to Brenda H who continues, on a daily basis, to do work behind the scenes. I can't wait to see you next year, so I can properly hug and thank you.

I also want to thank my parents for all the great discussions lately about my work and the art of creativity. Knowing how proud you are and the respect you have for my muses means a lot.

To all my fans who picked up Safe Haven and began the journey of Captain and Candy with me, thank you. Your enthusiastic support and reviews have touched me deeply. You make writing a beautiful experience.

SIGN UP FOR MY NEWSLETTER
HERE FOR THE LATEST RED
PHOENIX UPDATES

SALES, GIVEAWAYS, NEW
RELEASES, PREORDER LINKS, AND
MORE!

SIGN UP HERE

REDPHOENIXAUTHOR.COM/NEWSLETTER-
SIGNUP

CONTENTS

Painful Farewell 1

Unexpected Hello 8

Karma 17

Fate 24

His Proposal 32

Her Acceptance 49

The Protector 57

Trouper 76

The Mystery 89

Casualties 104

The Unexpected 115

The Mission 127

As One 141

Echo 153

Redemption 165

New Vision 174

Old Fears 183

Meeting Destiny 192

Understanding 211

Closure 223

Tribute..235

Full Circle 246

Coming Next..255

About the Author...257

Other Red Phoenix Books................................260

Connect with Red on Substance B 265

Painful Farewell

Captain

"Goodbye, my pet…"
I allow myself one last look in the rearview mirror as we drive away from each other. An overwhelming sadness threatens to devour me, and I force my gaze to return to the road straight ahead.

I hold onto the fact that I am doing the right thing for Candy, but I find myself reminded of a similar moment when I was young and felt bereft after being kicked out of my home. I was certain I was doing the right thing back then—but being right didn't make it hurt any less.

So, knowing I'm in for a bad night and in need of a friend, I drive straight to Gallant's place. It is unusual for me to visit unannounced, however, I trust he will understand.

Ena answers the door when I knock. Her eyes widen when she sees me, and she immediately bows her head. "What a lovely surprise, Captain." Stepping aside, she invites me into the house.

I nod curtly as I enter, too wound up in my emotions to speak. I'm surprised to see their two young girls running up, but they suddenly stop short when they see me. I have visited on several occasions, so they have no reason to be shocked by my face.

"Captain Walker," the oldest says in a voice filled with awe as she gives me a salute.

It isn't until then I realize that I still have my uniform on. Although the child's salute is unnecessary, I appreciate the sentiment behind the gesture and thank her.

The other little one smiles, adding, "You look so handsome, Mr. Walker."

I chuckle, knowing I look anything but. However, their youthful kindness tugs at my heart.

"Is that Captain's voice I hear?" Gallant asks from somewhere in the house. When he arrives and sees me in uniform, he instantly stands at attention.

I can't help but smirk, noting how old habits die hard.

"At ease," I mutter, shifting uncomfortably, wishing I had thought to take off my uniform before coming here.

Gallant eyes me thoughtfully before asking his wife, "Ena, would you please pour Captain and me a glass of Jack Daniels?"

"Of course," she answers. Ena artfully herds her children out of the room, apologizing as she leaves, "They know better than to stare, Captain Walker. Please accept my apologies."

I smile at the two young girls who continue to stare

at me.

"No need to apologize, Mrs. Gallant. I find your daughters' attention endearing."

Once the children are out of the room, Gallant puts his hand on my shoulder. "I'm glad you came."

I grunt in disagreement. "It was a foolish thing to do. I should leave."

"Nonsense!" he assures me, walking toward his study. "I consider it an honor you've come to visit."

I say nothing as I take a seat and wait for Ena to arrive with the drinks. Once she shuts the door behind her, I meet Gallant's gaze. "I'd like to know what you thought would happen when you advised me to bid for Candy at the auction."

Gallant sits back in his chair and smiles warmly, not concerned with the gruffness in my voice. "As I said at the time, I knew you would provide Miss Cox with the experience she needed."

I growl, "Did you not anticipate there would be complications?"

"Such as?"

"That the girl might come to have feelings for me?"

"I'm not surprised. I mentioned to you that I thought you two were a good match. I was perfectly clear about that when we spoke."

"Well, I never expected Candy to fall in love." I turn my head from him and mutter, "Or for me to feel the same for her."

His eyes light up in sudden understanding. "That's the reason for the uniform. You plan on collaring her today."

I look away, the pain of leaving her still too fresh to bear. I pick up the chilled glass of whiskey and look him in the eye. "Nope."

I watch as Gallant's brow furrows. "I'm clearly missing something here."

"I *was* going to collar her, but I just met her parents."

"What happened?" he asks with concern.

"They're a hell of a lot younger than I am. I felt like an old fool standing there." I stand up and start pacing. "What the hell is wrong with me? Thinking it could work between us?" I shake my head angrily, disgusted with myself. "Even worse, her poor mother couldn't bear to look at me—and for good reason. I have the face of a monster."

Gallant says nothing, a look of compassion on his face.

"So...rather than embarrass Candy, I left."

"How did Candy react to you leaving?" he asks, clearly concerned for his former student.

"She wasn't there, Gallant. Candy has no idea what I had planned for today." I turn away from him and shut my eye as the wave of grief settles over me.

"She must never know. It would break her heart."

"Do you honestly feel this is the right decision?"

I turn and snarl at him. "Was there ever any question? I've already lived the best years of my life. It's only downhill for me from here on out. While Candy...she's got her whole life ahead of her."

"Have you?" he asks in a demanding tone.

I look at him with resentment, in no mood for nonsensical questions. "Have I what?"

"Have you lived the best years of your life? Because I believe better ones are ahead."

I throw my hands up in frustration. "I need the support of a friend right now. Don't you dare make me starting doubting my decision."

Gallant stands up and walks over to me. "You were brutally frank with me once while I was under your command, so let me return the favor as your mentor. You maintain that Candy should commit to a younger Dom, while she insists otherwise."

I nod in agreement.

"As you are an honorable man, I know you would never purposely hurt Miss Cox."

"Of course."

"Since you have a clear difference of opinion with Candy, I suggest you put your assertion to the test. Give her a temporary collar and present her with Dominants you feel are worthy."

"Absolutely not!"

"Hear me out," Gallant insists, holding up his hand. "Acting as her temporary Dominant, you can set up opportunities for her to interact with Doms you deem better suited. If you are correct in your assertion, she will forge a greater connection with one or more of them, and you will be free to let her go without hurting her."

Although I can see the wisdom behind his suggestion, spending more time with Candy would make it far more painful when I finally have to let her go.

"On the flipside," Gallant states, "if no connections are made with the men you have specifically chosen, you must concede defeat and accept that you're wrong, presenting Miss Cox with the permanent collar you planned to give her."

I snort in disgust. "The test is unfair to her. I'm surprised you would even suggest it. Giving Candy the carrot of a temporary collar when we have no future together seems far crueler than simply walking away."

"Captain, I know you have the highest respect for Miss Cox, which is why you should give her the opportunity to decide for herself."

I let out a frustrated sigh, remembering the look on her mother's face and the humiliation I felt when her father tried to push cash into my hand. To subject myself to further insult just to prove to Candy that our relationship is doomed seems foolhardy at best.

However, Gallant is right about one thing. It would be far better for Candy to look back on our relationship years from now, having willingly walked away, than to nurse the festering wound of a broken heart.

"I will consider what you've said," I inform him, even though I dislike the suggestion.

"I'm glad to hear it."

"And, just for the record, you make a horrific matchmaker."

Gallant chuckles lightly. "I was simply trying to pair like partners for a scene—nothing more."

I snort, not believing him, as I set my glass down on the table. "I believe we are done here, and I can't say I particularly enjoyed our little talk."

"Funny, that's what I would have said after our conversation about my stature all those years ago."

"It wasn't your stature," I correct him. "It was your

lack of confidence that I took issue with."

Gallant tilts his head slightly. "I stand corrected."

As I leave, I notice Ena waiting at the door to see me out. "I hope you will come again soon, Captain Walker."

"Next time, let's make it my place. And bring the girls."

"Goodbye, Captain Walker!" the oldest calls out from the hallway.

I find myself smiling, despite everything that's happened. While I may be too old to have patience for most children, I have a definite soft spot for these two.

I turned to Gallant before heading out the door. "If I choose to go through with this test and I'm right, you're going to owe me."

"And, if it turns out you're wrong, I shall call in a favor at some point," he replies smoothly.

I chuckle on my way out.

Although the road ahead could prove precarious, at least I will have an end goal in mind by taking her on as a temporary sub. However, I refuse to dwell on the fact that completing such a mission would mark the official end of Candy and me.

Unexpected Hello

Candy

I park the car and pull numerous Christmas gifts out from the back seat. I can't explain it, but I am overwhelmed with a feeling of joy and chalk it up to the pure magic of the holiday season.

I love everything about Christmas—the music, the decorations, the holiday treats and, of course, the gifts—especially when you find *just* the right one.

I can't wait for Captain to open the special one I bought today!

I head up the stairs to my apartment and pause at the door, struck by the faint scent of Captain's cologne. When I hear movement inside my apartment, I smile to myself, knowing he's come to surprise me.

I get my keys out to unlock the door and slowly open it, trying to keep a casual look on my face as I walk inside.

My jaw drops when I see who is waiting for me inside. Instead of Captain, my mom and dad are standing there.

"Hi, honey," my mom says, as if being here is completely normal.

I stare blankly at the two of them, unable to process that they're here and not Captain.

"I think we broke Cleopatra with our surprise," my dad jokes, waving his hand in front of my face.

I shake my head and laugh, trying to regain my composure. "Sorry. It's just that I thought I smelled something…" My voice trails off, realizing I was mistaken. Not wanting to explain myself, I ask Dad, "What's up with this sudden visit? Is everything okay?"

My mom walks over, pinching my cheeks gently. "Everything's fine, honey. We just couldn't stand the idea of our little girl being alone for Christmas, so we decided to surprise you as our gift."

I take her hands from my cheeks and squeeze them, taking a step back. I hide my disappointment, not wanting to hurt their feelings.

As much as I love my parents, I was really counting on spending Christmas alone with Captain. "You definitely surprised me…"

"We can see that," my dad says with a cheerful laugh. "I want you to know we didn't come empty-handed, C. We've gone all out for you." He unzips one of their suitcases, pointing to the all the DVDs crammed inside. "I've brought all the holiday classics, so we can binge while we munch on your mother's peppermint popcorn."

My mom clasps her hands together excitedly. "I've brought all the ingredients to make our favorite holiday treat." She unzips a bigger suitcase to show off every-thing she's brought. "It's going to be just like old times, Cleo!"

I'm so used to being called Candy these days that hearing my old name throws me. I repeat her words, trying to mirror her excitement. "Yeah, just like old times…"

Considering the dark times we've experienced as a family, it astounds me how strong my parents seem now. According to my dad, Mom hasn't had an episode longer than a couple of days since that first night I called them from the Submissive Training Center.

My parents still have no idea what happened with Liege, blindly accepting my story of needing to unplug from the pressures of college over Spring Break and running off to the beaches of California. I told them that after immersing myself in the healing power of the sun and waves, I couldn't bear returning to that university.

They were understandably angry, not about my deci-sion to drop out of college, but in my failure to call them. They will never know what really happened those weeks that I went missing. Telling them about Liege would not have brought me any comfort, and it would have devastated them both.

Who knows what might happen to Mom if she knew.

Thankfully, despite their anger with me for making them worry, and after hearing my voice and knowing I was safe, my parents chose to forgive me—but only after I swore never to disappear again.

That is one promise I have no trouble keeping.

I glance at my dad and can see a marked difference in his physical appearance. Not having to care for my mother on a daily basis seems to have given him new life. He looks years younger.

Although my parents' visit is unexpected, I'm touched that they came all this way on a whim. I stave off the feeling of disappointment even as the hint of Captain's cologne still haunts me.

Oh, Captain…

Deciding to accept this sudden change of plans, I look down at the bags I'm holding and announce, "I'll go hide these and get the spare room ready for you guys."

"I'd be happy to help," my mom offers.

"Nope, you get started on the popcorn, Mom. That's your only focus right now."

I head to my bedroom and set the bags down, pulling my cell phone from out of my purse.

I immediately dial Captain's number, wanting to hear his voice and explain that I have unexpected guests I want to introduce him to. Unfortunately, he doesn't pick up right away. Rather than leave a message, I hang up and send him a text.

Tried to call. Parents surprised me with a visit. Would love for you to meet them. Does tonight work?

I figure there's no reason to put off introductions. I love Captain, and my parents need to meet the man who has totally captured my heart.

Do I think they will be shocked?

Yes—at first. Who wouldn't be with the age difference and his war wounds? But, once they get to know Captain, they'll feel differently. I'm sure of it.

I grab fresh sheets out of the closet and make the bed for them, checking my phone several times while I work, hoping to hear back from him.

Before I leave the spare room, I set my phone to vibrate and slip it into my pocket so I won't miss his response.

"Is it okay with you guys if I invite someone over for dinner tonight? I'd really like you to meet him."

Dad gives me a knowing look. "A new boyfriend for me to grill?"

"Are you really dating someone, Cleo?" my mom asks.

"I am, and he's perfect."

"More perfect than Ethan?" I can hear the surprise in Dad's voice.

I lean in close to him. "Not more than Ethan. But definitely on the same level."

"Oh, I'm so happy for you, sweetie. I can't wait to meet him," my mom cries.

"I'm happy for you, too, C. However, I will not spare him on the grilling."

I laugh. "I think he's more than man enough to handle it, Dad."

"So, how did you meet?" my mom asks, elbowing me.

I blush when I tell them. "We met at a pet shop, actually. He was looking for a kitten."

"Oh, that's so adorable! You can always trust a man

who's kind to animals," Mom tells Dad.

I try not to giggle.

Oh, he's more than just kind…

"Does he know about Ethan?" Dad asks. His fatherly concern over this new man in my life is easy to read.

"He does, Dad. And Charles totally accepts my feelings for Ethan and isn't threatened by them."

"It takes maturity to understand such a thing," my dad replies with an approving smile. "I can't help but like the guy already. Most men couldn't handle competing with a ghost."

I grin as I tell him, "Thankfully, Charles isn't the jealous type and would never ask me to forget Ethan. It's part of the reason he's so darn perfect."

"I hate to break it to you, sweetheart, but no one is perfect," my mom says.

I chuckle, shaking my head in disagreement. "I trust my instincts, Mom. In every way that matters, he's perfect."

"Well, you certainly got it right when you picked Ethan," my dad replies. "The fact is, you wouldn't be here today if it weren't for his quick thinking and courage."

I suck in a breath, feeling a fiery stab to my chest.

Ethan's gone because of me…

No matter how much time passes, I don't think I will ever get over the guilt.

My mom realizes Dad's comment has inadvertently hurt me, and she immediately apologizes for him. "Your father didn't mean to upset you, Cleo."

"I know." I give my Dad a sad smile. "No matter

how much it hurts sometimes, I don't want Ethan to be forgotten. Never apologize for mentioning him or sharing a memory. It's important to me."

My dad puts his arm around my shoulder and squeezes me against him. "Ethan is and will remain a part of our lives. That will never change—no matter how many years pass."

I take great comfort in his promise.

Pulling my mother and me into a three-way hug, my dad declares. "This is going to be a Cox Christmas to be remembered."

I nod excitedly, grateful that Captain will be a part of those memories.

With the mood lightened, Mom takes over my small kitchen to start on the popcorn while Dad has me go through all the films to pick the first movie for our binge.

I choose *The Gathering* as the official start to this Christmas season. I love the simple heart behind the film. A family broken by events from their past find a way back to each other through the simple magic of the season, bringing them together at a time of impending loss.

I always liked the movie as a teenager, but it means so much more to me now.

"I wish Ethan could have watched this with us," I mutter, laying my head against my dad's shoulder. I grab a handful of Mom's Christmas popcorn from the bowl when she settles down next to me on the couch.

"He's here," my mom assures me, placing a small bowl of popcorn on the coffee table. She smiles at my puzzled look and answers, "For Ethan."

I sigh in approval, holding up a handful of the tasty treat in honor of Ethan.

The three of us watch the beginning of the film in silence, settling into the familiar storyline like a warm blanket. I hold back the tears as the father learns he only has a few months to live. A part of me is jealous he has so much time to say goodbye when Ethan didn't have any—not even a second.

It's silly to feel jealous of a character in a movie…but I can't help it.

"Too much for you?" my mom asks, looking at me with concern.

"C's just fine," Dad says. "She picked this movie for a reason." He pats me on the shoulder as he returns his attention back to the screen.

My mom adjusts her position on the couch and pretends not to worry about me. I know she means well, but her constant fretting only makes me feel worse.

I turn my head toward my father and mouth the word, "Thanks."

We watch as each person in the family struggles to reconcile, fighting to find a way back to each other. This particular Christmas story has all the feels because the people and their struggles are so real, but it's the love and strength of their family that prevails.

Tears of gratitude flow down my cheeks at the end, and I look at my parents, smiling through happy tears. "I love you both so much."

I get a hug from both sides, and I am overwhelmed with a feeling of contentment. There is such a deep and abiding power found in family.

It makes me think of Captain, who had had that stolen from him as a young man. Although he has shared that his father disowned him, Captain has shared very little else about his past. I hope, with time, he will learn to trust me and open up.

However, I'm not just curious about his father. I want to know what happened with his mother and brother when he returned home wounded, still fighting for his life. Plus, there's the mystery man named Grapes. What role did he play in Captain's life?

I look at my father. The gratitude I feel for him is so intense, it almost hurts. "Thank you for always loving and supporting me, Dad."

"How could I not?" he answers. "You're my daughter."

I turn my head and tell Mom, "Thank you for not giving in to the darkness. I couldn't bear to ever lose you."

Mom's lips tremble slightly when she smiles. Her tender gaze moves from me to Dad. "Your father is my hero. He's never given up on me. Never stopped loving me through all of the years of depression and meds."

"You're my Irish Rose, Katherine. I would do anything for you," he tells her.

Their love is the kind of love I feel for Captain. That's why I am determined to convince that man to collar me.

I glance at my phone, worried that I haven't heard from him yet. Normally, Captain is quick to answer.

"Hey, Mom, why don't you pick the next movie?"

The twinkle I see in her eye makes me smile. I haven't seen that spark in a very long time...

16

Karma

Captain

Returning home, I immediately take off my uniform. I hang the jacket back up in the very back of the closet, unsure if I will ever have an occasion to wear it again—at least, until the day they bury my corpse in the ground.

I look down at the cluster of grapes tattooed on my wrist. It's hard to believe how many years it's been since Grapes died. I feel a rush of emotion, remembering the day he was laid to rest. I am instantly transported back to that time.

Soon after receiving the long-awaited news that Grapes' remains had finally been located and recovered from a mass grave, I was told they were being transported back to the U.S. Unfortunately, his family refused to accept his body, so arrangements were made for him to be buried with a military honors service in the Los Angeles National Cemetery.

Although I am thoroughly disgusted by his parents' response, I'm also secretly grateful for the decision to bury him in Los Angeles. I need a physical location to mourn my friend.

It is a place I visit often…

Knowing the volatile history Grapes had with his family, I send a letter to his parents. In that letter, I not only list his many accomplishments during his distinguished military career, I also share who Grapes was as a man, because it seems his family never knew him.

He told me that when he was growing up, his mother reminded him on a daily basis that she wished he'd never been born, and his father took it one step further by physically torturing him for being a burden to them.

Somehow, despite the horrific childhood he suffered, Grapes was able to transcend his piss-poor upbringing and become a man of honor. I wanted—no I *needed*— them to know that they hadn't broken him.

I end the letter detailing the date and time of his burial. In my eyes, it's the last chance they have to redeem themselves.

I dress in full uniform to attend his graveside service. Not one of his family comes and attendance is small because most of the men who knew him well died on the battlefield with him that same day. That weighs heavy on my soul.

Grapes receives military honors, and I take comfort in the tradition, hearing the honor guard firing the three volleys from their rifles, along with the forlorn rendition of "Taps" and the ceremonial folding of the flag.

Because none of his kin are present, I am handed the flag that covered his coffin and told, "On behalf of the President of the United States, the United States Army, and a grateful nation, please accept this flag as a symbol of our appreciation for Warrant Officer Bell's honorable and faithful service."

My throat clenches up, making it impossible to speak, but I nod as I take the flag from the man.

I go home that day angry that his parents never paid him the slightest amount of respect, not even in death. I find, as time goes on, that I become more and more incensed.

There comes a point when I can no longer let what happened to Grapes go. I've become obsessed, and I have to do something—not only in retribution for Grapes, but for my own sanity.

I make a personal trip to his hometown and head directly to the house where Grapes grew up. I'm not surprised to find the house lacks any evidence of upkeep or care.

I walk to the door and knock hard.

I hear voices inside, but no one comes to answer the door, so I knock again with more urgency.

Finally, a burst of foul language erupts as an angry man on the other side of the door slowly makes his way over to open it. He takes his time undoing the lock, before opening the door just a crack and peeking through the screen door.

"Oh, my God," he shouts behind him. "It's another

one of them in a monkey suit, but this one is messed up."

To me he says, "Why don't you military fuckers leave us the hell alone?" He slams the door on me before I can reply.

That's okay, I decide.

I don't need to speak.

I head back to my car and lay out a set of civilian clothes from my suitcase. Driving to the nearest gas station, I change in the restroom. I don't want to represent the Army knowing what I'm about to do.

Returning to the house, I knock again. I'm there a full ten minutes, hitting the door with my fists, before he finally answers again.

I already have the screen door open, so as soon as he opens the door a crack, I push against it, causing it to swing wide open.

He stands there, sputtering, while a scrawny woman rushes to the door with a baseball bat clutched in her hands, and threatens me.

"Get far away from us, mister!" She raises the wooden bat as if to strike me.

I ignore her, glaring at the man with disdain, "If it were legal, I would do to you what you did to your own son as a child. But, what you did *isn't* legal, and you should be in jail."

The woman spits at me angrily. "Adam got what he deserved. That little fuck was nothing but a troublemaker."

The man beside her snorts with amusement. "And now that worthless piece of shit is less than nothing.

He's fucking dirt."

I only see red.

Cocking my fist back, I let him have it square in the nose. The man squawks like a bird as his hands fly up to his face.

I watch as his nose begins spurting large amounts of blood, much to my satisfaction.

"That fucker broke my nose! The one-eyed monkey just broke my nose!"

The rush of blood pounds in my head as my rage builds but, somewhere deep within, I feel a check in my spirit. It is the only thing that stops me from totally going off on the man.

Instead, I forced myself to take a step back, not trusting myself. "Adam Bell was the finest man I ever knew, *and* he was my best friend." My voice strains with emotion as I speak the truth. "I thank God he walked away from you two. You aren't fit to lick his boots."

The woman howls in anger, trying to take a swing at me with her bat, but I easily pull it from her grasp and throw it to the floor.

"I'm calling the cops!" the man shouts between his bloody hands.

"Do," I challenge, certain he won't. "I suspect pressing burning cigarettes into the skin of a child isn't the only law you've broken."

"Motherfucker!" he cries, charging me.

I dart out of the way and gave him a push as he passes by. The man tumbles off his broken porch and lands face first in the dirt.

The woman screeches in rage, but I turn to her with

my fists in the air. "I have no qualms about hitting abusive mothers."

She hesitates for a moment, choosing to rush past me to grab her husband, who is floundering in the dirt. She starts dragging him back toward the house, looking at me warily.

"You should have made amends with your son when he was still alive."

She stares at me for a moment, but says nothing before she disappears into the house.

"You're just a one-eyed fuck," the man growls as his wife lets go of him and he stumbles into the doorway.

I see the perfect opportunity and can't pass it up…

"I hope to hell karma bites you in the ass," I say as I plant my boot on his butt and push.

I walk away, listening to their violent curses. I don't know how Grapes ever survived these two, but I look up at the sky and smile.

"That last part? That was for you, buddy."

I hang up my slacks, sliding them to the back beside the jacket, before shutting the closet door. I feel a sense of regret. Had things gone according to plan, Candy would be here now, wearing her pretty new collar around her neck.

Instead, I am here alone, but by my own choice.

I wander aimlessly through the house, contemplating my next plan of action.

I personally believe it's best to end things with Candy now, because it would allow her to move on, and I feel for both our sakes that the sooner that happens, the better.

However, I loathe the idea of breaking her heart, and I know if I leave her, she will never understand.

I curse fate for the thirty-six years between us.

But, I know it is foolish to dwell on things I cannot change. So, here I am, faced with a difficult dilemma.

Do I break Candy's heart now or do I allow her to break mine later?

Fate

Candy

After a quick dinner, the three of us settle in for another movie. It begins with a scene of a man ringing a bell for the Salvation Army.

"Hey, that reminds me of that man who came by earlier today."

I look at my mom questioningly. "What man?"

"A wounded warrior who came by to collect money for the charity," my dad answers.

Goosebumps rise on my skin, but I try to sound nonchalant when I ask him, "What do you mean?"

My mother answers for him. "There was this poor military guy with an eye patch who came to your door. You'll be pleased to know your father gave a generous amount."

"Of course. We gladly support our military and I was more than happy to give," my dad states proudly.

I feel the blood drain from my face.

I wasn't imagining things when I smelled Captain's

cologne. I want to die, imagining the humiliation he must have felt when my parent answered the door and tried to give him money.

It suddenly strikes me that he must have been wearing his uniform for them to know he was part of the military. I swallow hard. That could only mean one thing...

I slap my hands to my face, dragging them down in frustration.

Whatever he wanted was extremely important. Was he going to collar me?

"Mom. Dad. I have to go," I tell them, jumping off the couch.

"What? You have to be kidding, sweetie. We have the entire night planned," my mother says, laughing.

"It has something to do with that man who came to the door, doesn't it?" my Dad says. "We were mistaken about him."

I only nod vigorously, unwilling to waste another second. "I'll explain everything, but I need to leave—now."

"But, sweetheart, the movie already started. Surely, it can wait just a couple of hours," my mother begs.

"No, it can't, Mom. This most definitely can't wait."

My dad can tell how concerned I am and tells me, "C, if we upset the man in any way, please tell him it was unintentional."

I close my eyes, just imagining the mortifying scene playing out in my mind.

Poor Captain...

I definitely can't get there soon enough, so I race toward the door with just my purse, telling them, "I'll be back as soon as I can."

"But, Cleo!" my mom protests.

"Let her be, Katherine," my dad scolds her gently. "I think we made a mess of things."

I wipe away the tears and race to his house. I can't help wondering if Captain came to present me with a collar. Why else would he come dressed in his uniform?

And…how was he greeted? Oh, my goodness!

I know my parents meant well, but I cannot begin to fathom what went through Captain's head when they answered the door and threw cash at him.

No wonder he hasn't been answering my calls…

Once I pull up to his home, I see right away that none of the lights are on, but that doesn't stop me from ringing his doorbell and knocking repeatedly.

"Please, please, please answer…" I cry.

Finally, I have to accept that he isn't home, but I'm *desperate* to find him.

It's imperative.

I know he has been spending more time with Baron lately and pin my hopes on the belief that that's where he is.

Without bothering to call, I head to Baron's apartment. If Captain is there, after the humiliation he just faced at the hands of my parents, I don't want to chance him slipping out the back to avoid talking to me.

I pull up and jump out of my car, literally running to the door. I start ringing the doorbell, and I'm still gasping for breath when Baron answers.

The impressive Dom chuckles when his sees me.

"Let me guess. You're looking for Captain."

"Is he here?" I crane my neck to look around him, hoping to catch sight of Captain.

"No. I'm sorry to disappoint you, Miss Cox. He came by several hours ago to tell me that I am free to pursue you."

I'm crushed and lean against the doorway for support. "But…I don't understand. I thought…"

"Why don't we talk about it inside?" Baron suggests.

"You don't understand, Baron. I *have* to find Captain. What you just said proves it. Do you have any idea where he might be?"

Baron only shakes his head. "I haven't a clue where he went."

"Something unfortunate happened, and it's imperative I talk to him tonight."

He gives me a warm smile in response to how distressed I am. "If you are concerned about Captain's state of mind, don't be. He seemed quite level-headed when we spoke."

"Well, *I* won't be until I have a chance to talk to him." I sigh in frustration, not knowing where else to go. "Please, let me know if you hear from him."

"I'll be sure to tell Captain you're looking for him when we cross paths."

"Thank you!"

I get back in my car, wondering where he would have gone after talking to Baron. I drive to all the places Captain has taken me in the past, including the pet shop where we first met and the BDSM club, The Haven.

But, Captain is nowhere to be found. It's as if he's

disappeared. I finally give up and return to his place. My heart leaps with joy when I see a single light on in his home.

With my heart beating crazily, I ring the doorbell and wait. When he doesn't answer, I knock softly. "Captain, I need to speak with you."

My heart starts racing again when I hear the sound of his boots clicking on the hardwood floor as he approaches the door, but...

He does not open it.

Instead, I hear him say, "Go home, Candy."

I gasp and sniffle, "Please, Captain."

"It's been a long day. Go home. We will talk later."

"No, I need to talk to you *now*. Please."

"Candy, I'm in no mood to speak. Go home."

I close my eyes, wondering if I have lost him forever.

I can't accept that.

"Captain, you know my desire is to please you, but I cannot obey that command. I will sit out here all night, if I have to."

"Go home," he states again just before the receding sound of his boots echo down the hallway.

I turn my back against the door and slowly slide down it. I know Captain is a stubborn soul, but so am I.

Captain was *this* close to accepting the two of us. We were almost there...and I'm convinced I'm right. I am not willing to give up on us.

I look up at the night sky, silently cursing fate.

Of all the days for my parents to visit...

I don't want them worrying about me, so I give Dad a quick call. "Hey, just wanted to check in and let you know I'm fine, but that I might not be back for a while so don't wait up."

"C, do you want to tell me what this is all about?"

I hesitate, having planned to tell him with Captain present, but I don't have the luxury now. "Dad, the military officer you met this afternoon is my boyfriend."

"But the man we saw was way too old for you."

"Yes, Charles is older. But he's also the most honorable man I know, and I love him, Dad. You might not believe it now, but once you have a chance to know him, you'll agree he's the best man for me."

"But, C, he looks older than *we* are."

"He is, Dad. It's the reason he refuses to make a commitment even though I can't imagine my life without him."

"It's not only the age difference, C. It's obvious the man has medical issues."

"Actually, those are old war wounds that have healed. Charles is every bit as fit and strong as you are."

There's a long silence but I don't press him to speak, knowing I've given him a lot to take in.

"Where are you now?" he finally asks.

"I'm waiting to talk to Captain."

I blush, realizing I've just called him by his Dom name in front of my dad. I quickly amend my error by explaining, "His full name is Captain Charles Walker."

"What?" he asks, sounding surprise.

"His name is Captain Charles Walker," I repeat. "Why? What's up?"

"I have a strange feeling I might know this man, but I can't place how. Still, the name seems awfully familiar to me…" His voice trails off for a moment, then he adds, "I won't lie, C. I'm uncertain how I feel about you dating someone so much older than you."

"I knew this wouldn't be easy for you or Mom. But there's honestly nothing you can say to dissuade me from loving him. Believe me, Captain's tried hard enough."

"I'll hold my judgement until I've had a chance to speak with him. I think it would be best if I break this gently to your mother before you return. What she didn't tell you is that she was scared of him because of…his scars."

I feel my stomach twist into a knot. Yet another humiliation Captain had to endure. "Well, I'm sure she'll get over that once she gets to know him." I can't hide the anger in my voice, upset that my own mother treated Captain that way.

"C, you can't hold it against her. It was purely an instinctual reaction. She wasn't trying to be rude."

"Dad, it's important that you and Mom be honest tomorrow when you talk to him, but, no matter *what*, you have to look him in the eye. He deserves that respect."

"Point taken. I'll make sure to mention that to your mother."

"Dad, this isn't just a simple fling for me. Charles is the man I love."

Hanging up the phone, I feel better after speaking with my father. However, I have no illusions that this is going to be easy for my parents.

Even so, I would rather face this head-on as a family than pussyfoot around Captain's age.

It's my hope that when Captain sees how serious I

am about bringing him into my family, he'll finally accept that I believe in our future together. This isn't a crush; this is full-on love.

I'm all in.

With that in mind, I curl up against his door and settle in for the night. I know Captain is as bullheaded as I am. It's part of the reason I love him so much.

At exactly midnight, I hear the lock disengage and I push myself away from the door as it slowly opens. I look up into Captain's sad face, and can tell he's been suffering.

Looking down at me, he shakes his head. "What am I going to do with you, pet?"

His Proposal

Captain

I look at Candy curled up on my doorstep, and it takes everything in me not to gather her into my arms and profess my love to her.

I can't fathom how I've earned the devotion of someone as beautiful and true as Candy. It seems impossible, and yet, here she is—that stubborn little soul, lying on the cold concrete of my front step.

I hold out my hand to her. "Come."

Her face lights up and for an instant I feel uneasy, knowing the end goal of my mission. However, I love this girl too much not to go through with it now.

She has not only captured my heart, but my undying loyalty.

I lead her into the house and head toward the formal living room. It's obvious she's heard of my visit from her parents, which is why she's insistent that we talk.

I make a warm fire to take the chill from her bones. Looking back at Candy, her eyes full of hope and love, I silently pray Gallant's suggestion will ensure her heart is protected. It is the only reason to go through with this plan.

My mission is to find her a suitable partner and relieve her heart of the burden that my age and condition brings.

Listening to the crackling fire, I envision a day when I may be invited to a holiday gathering with Candy six months pregnant with a second child. The little girl, who is her spitting image, jumps up and down when she sees me, crying, "Uncle Charles...!"

That is a dream I think on often and the goal I aspire to when I sit down beside Candy to explain my objective.

"I am considering the idea of a temporary collar."

I see the joy on her face and immediately add, "But this would only be until I find you a suitable partner."

Her expression instantly changes, and then I see it....a flash of pain that clouds those beautiful eyes.

Oh, fuck. What have I done?

I forge on, because I believe in my mission and I will not fail her.

"Candy, if you were to agree to wear this collar," I say, pulling a plain black leather collar from my pocket and holding it up to her to see. "I would commit to finding a Dom worthy of you."

"But..."

"You know how I feel about our future," I remind her gently.

Her eyes remain fixed on the simple collar I hold as I continue to explain, "As my temporary submissive, you would be committing to giving each man I select a fair

33

chance. There's no point in this temporary partnership unless you promise to keep an open mind—and heart. This isn't about us. This is about you."

She stares hard at the collar for several moments before asking, "What if I still choose you after interacting with the Doms you have chosen? Will you agree to collar me then?"

I frown, afraid she is missing the point. "This will only work if you fully commit. Pretending to comply in the hopes that I will eventually collar you will only result in me dismissing this entire arrangement and walking away."

"I understand, Captain," she answers respectfully. "But, by the same token, I cannot choose someone else simply because you believe I should."

"I agree, pet. I would never force you into a partnership that is not of your choosing."

"So, I ask again, Captain. If no other Dom earns my submission, will I wear your permanent collar after this temporary partnership ends, or will you abandon me?"

As hardened as I am, I cringe at her last words. I never want to be a source of her pain.

"Pet, if we both agree that our partnership benefits us at the end of the trial period, I will claim you in a private collaring ceremony. However, there would be one stipulation I'd insist upon."

"What is it?" she asks, her voice tinged with apprehension.

"If, at any time, you find a better-suited Master, I will release you."

She frowns. "Wouldn't that make that collar temporary as well? My desire is to be permanently collared."

I reach out and caress her cheek. "*If* I were to claim you as my own, I would remain fully committed to you—always. It would simply change to a different capacity should you find a better-suited Dom later on."

"Captain, such an arrangement would be completely unfair to you."

"Pet, my deepest desire, as well as the end goal here, is to see you happy."

She gives me a troubled look, clearly concerned for my wellbeing.

I smile in response to her concern, confident with my decision. "Will you agree to this arrangement?"

Her gaze returns to the collar in my hand before she looks up at me. "I would be honored to wear your temporary collar, Captain, and I will accept the conditions behind it, fully committing to each encounter you present to me."

"Good. We won't officially begin until after Christmas. Right now, I want you to spend your time with your parents without any distractions. Your family has come a long way to see you."

She stares at the collar in my hand, a look of longing in her eyes as I put it back in my pocket. Accepting that she must wait, she says, "I thank you for your thoughtfulness toward my parents, and I humbly ask if you will consider joining us for dinner tomorrow."

I balk at the invitation, remembering how her mother couldn't bear to look at me. Dinner with her parents would be an awkward evening, at best. "Pet, I'm sure they need time to adjust before we actually meet face to face again."

She takes my hand in hers, looking up at me with those big, round doe-like eyes. "I can't wait to introduce you to them properly. Please say you'll come."

I groan inwardly, dreading the idea after our disastrous initial encounter. But, as I gaze into her trusting eyes, I know I cannot disappoint her. If this woman wants me to meet her parents, it is my honor to do so—no matter how excruciating the evening may be.

"I will join you for dinner tomorrow. What time?"

"Seven would be perfect!"

Her enthusiasm belies the nature of tomorrow's encounter. This isn't a simple dinner. This is a confrontation, and I will be the main event.

So be it.

No matter what happens tomorrow, Candy's welfare remains my foremost concern. If things should get too volatile, I will simply leave and, by doing so, defuse the situation.

I arrive promptly at seven, dressed in a simple black suit. I adjust my eye patch and let out a stressed sigh before knocking on the door.

Candy answers it immediately, swinging the door wide open. Taking my hand with a huge smile on her face, she pulls me inside. "I'm so happy you came!"

Both of her parents are waiting for me as I walk in. The room instantly fills with an uncomfortable silence as her father looks me over with a critical eye. I notice her mother's eyes darting around nervously, uncertain where to look. It's obvious my scars still make her uneasy, but she is trying to pretend otherwise.

"Mom, Dad, this is Charles."

I hold out my hand to them. "It is a pleasure to meet you both."

Her dad takes my hand and shakes it firmly, "I want you to know we didn't realize who you were before..."

"Understood," I reply curtly, not wanting to talk about our first encounter.

I turn toward her mother and gently take her trembling hand. She blushes profusely, her gaze dropping to the floor. "Mr. Walker."

I glance at Candy, giving her a slight smile. Yep, this is going as well as I expected.

"Charles, can I get you something to drink?" Candy asks.

What I'd really love is to down a fifth of Jack right now, but I answer, "Water, please."

"Why don't you all sit down while I get a round of water for everyone?"

"I'll help you, sweetie," her mother immediately answers, scooting off toward the kitchen.

I take a seat across from Mr. Cox. "I assume you have questions you'd like to ask me."

"I do." He looks at me with an odd expression for a moment, before asking, "Why did you get involved with our daughter when she's so much younger than you?"

"Dad!" Candy cries from the kitchen.

I hold up my hand, telling her, "He has every right to

ask."

Looking her father in the eye, I answer as truthfully as I can without exposing our BDSM ties. Because my age and condition are enough of a barrier at this point, I don't want to bring our kink into the mix and muddy the waters further.

"A friend set us up on a blind date. I obviously noted the significant age difference, but, as it was only one evening, we both decided to enjoy each other's company and found we had a lot in common."

Candy walks into the room, handing a glass of water to me first before giving one to her father.

He takes a drink from the glass and sets it down before asking me, "Why continue dating?"

"As I said, we had more in common than either of us expected. I didn't see it as dating so much as spending time with Candy." I look at her and smile. "She's an extraordinary person."

"I agree my daughter is amazing, but I can't help being concerned that a man over thirty years her senior wants to date her."

I put down my glass and look at both her parents. "I completely agree that my age precludes me from having a serious relationship with her."

Candy lets out a small whimper, tears welling up in her eyes as she takes a quick sip from her glass. She blinks the tears away before her parents notice.

"Are you saying that you do not love our daughter, when it's obvious to us how deeply she cares for you?" her mother asks accusingly. "Because it would be cruel to toy with her feelings like that, Mr. Walker."

"Mrs. Cox, for better or worse, I have fallen in love with Candy over the course of our time together." I meet her mother's heated gaze. "It's because of my feelings for Candy that I am determined to do right by her. But, I'm sure you are aware that your daughter is a very stubborn woman."

Mr. Cox chuckles. "She takes after the Cox's side in that regard."

"I've tried to persuade her to find someone else, but I have been highly unsuccessful."

"But do you love her enough that you are willing to let her go?" her mother prods.

"Yes."

Candy lets out a growl of frustration this time. "Why does everyone ignore what I want? I understand there is a huge age gap between us, but in every way that matters, Charles is what I need. I love him just as fiercely as I did Ethan."

She turns to her father. "You didn't question my feelings then. Why don't you trust me now?"

"It's only natural that we are concerned for you, C," he answers.

"Dad, trust me when I say I love Charles just as deeply as I do Ethan. I'm not looking to marry. I just need you to treat us like a couple, because that's what we are."

"Are you planning on moving in together?" Candy's mother asks her.

I clear my throat. "Actually, we haven't discussed that. At this point, Candy's seeking a relationship and nothing more."

"Is that true, Cleo?"

"Yes, I just want to be free to love Charles, and for him to love me. All I need from you is to respect us as a couple. That's it."

Mr. Cox looks me over again, his expression solemn. "You'll be good to my daughter?"

"I promise to treat her with love and respect."

"You better not break her heart or you'll have me to answer to," her mother states, her eyes flashing with the fierceness of a mother bear.

I'm charmed by her mother's protective nature. "Mrs. Cox, I can assure you that when Candy is ready to move on, I will let her go with a full heart. I'm sincere when I say I want what is best for her."

Her mother glances over at her husband in surprise.

"Do you mind if we talk privately?" her father asks.

"By all means. If it would make things easier for you, I'd be happy to leave."

"No, that's not necessary."

After they shut the door to the guest room, Candy shakes her head at me. "I don't know whether to hug you or to be mad at you."

"Why?" I ask, feeling things have gone exceedingly well so far.

"I don't like hearing you tell them that you will let me go when the time comes. But...my heart burst with happiness when you declared your love for me in front of my parents."

"I'll admit the conversation hasn't gone the way I envisioned. I was expecting accusations or, at the very least, an undercurrent of hostility from your parents."

"I didn't. You are an incredible man, and they can see that."

"What I see is your parents' love and support for you, my pet."

Taking my hand, she squeezes it tightly. "It's normal for parents to love their children unconditionally."

I shake my head, my personal experience having been the opposite. However, I am inspired by the love and understanding Candy's parents have shown her.

When Mr. and Mrs. Cox step out of the back bedroom a short time later, I note the serious expressions on their faces. I'm not surprised they still have concerns.

"Nothing is off limits," I assure them as they sit down.

"I have a personal question," her mother begins.

"Ask away."

She touches the side of her cheek. "How did…?"

Although the question is not unexpected, it's a topic I do not care to talk about, so I keep my answer brief. "A grenade exploded near my head."

"You're lucky to be alive," she states.

"I lost too many men on that day to consider myself lucky, but you're right. It's a miracle I survived."

She looks at my face, trying to hide her discomfort. "I don't know how you cope after losing an eye and being so severely disfigured."

Candy stares at her in shock. "Mom."

I'm not easily offended and answer, gesturing to my face, "This is nothing. What's impossible to live with are the number of men I lost. It's because of them that I face each day, Mrs. Cox. I live to honor their sacrifice."

I'm overwhelmed by grief and have to look away before she notices the tear in my eye.

It never gets easier—*never.*

"Charles, I'm going to be blunt with you, and I expect an honest answer," her father states.

"Of course."

"Are you the reason my daughter quit college?"

"No. In fact, I plan to assist her in getting that marketing degree she's been working toward. Candy is far too intelligent to waste her talents serving food to diners."

"We're agreed on that."

"Charles, I can't let you do that," Candy protests, unaware of my plans since this is the first time I have spoken of them.

I chuckle, telling her, "Yes, you can. I socked away college money for my little brother, but he never used it. That money still sits in that savings account, benefiting no one."

"But you should buy something nice for yourself," she insists.

"A college education is what it was set aside for, and it's the best use for the money. It's not even a question for me."

"Wait a sec..." her father says. "You have a little brother? His name wouldn't happen to be Jacob?"

"It is." I look at him strangely, unnerved that he should know my brother's name.

"I'm finally starting to put the pieces together. I told C your name sounds familiar, so let me ask—you wouldn't happen to be Charles Walker, the big track star turned war hero of Riley High?"

Candy's eyes light up. "Oh, my goodness, Dad! I passed his picture in the display case every day going to lunch. I can't believe I didn't recognize the resemblance until now."

I look at Candy in disbelief. "Are you telling me you graduated from the same high school I did?"

"Not only C, but myself, as well," her father informs me.

I shake my head, stunned by the revelation.

"The principal highly respected you, and he often said you were the finest graduate to come out of Riley High. He held you up as a prime example of the extraordinary power resolve can have in the face of adversity."

"But, why me? I was nothing special."

"You're being too modest. Principal Hall shared how his brother met you at the bus station just as you were leaving for boot camp. Your determination and love of country left quite an impression on him."

"Officer Hall…" I see the face of the security officer in my mind as clearly if he is standing in front of me right now. "He gave me a meal the night before I left and stayed to see me off the next morning when I headed out." I am moved by the memory and share, "He'll never know what his compassion meant to me."

"Well, now that I know who you are, I need to shake your hand again." Her father stands up and holds his hand out to me. "It is an honor to meet you in person, Captain Charles Walker."

Candy joins him, her eyes sparkling with pride. "I bet you didn't know you're an inspiration to future alumni."

A chill of providence washes over me as I look at her. It is strange to think we haunted the halls of Riley High at different points in time. I can imagine Candy walking into class as I walk out, both of us passing each other, but unaware of each other's presence—thirty-six years separating us.

Her father asks, "Have you ever considered going back to speak at the high school, Mr. Walker? I'm sure you would be well received."

"To be brutally frank, the town holds bad memories for me. I vowed never to go back." I shudder just thinking about it. Not only is my father still there, but so is my ex-fiancé.

"That's a shame," Candy tells me. "I would love to be there when you speak at our old high school. Maybe it's time you return."

I fold my arms, shaking my head. "No."

"How can you dismiss the idea so quickly?" her mother cries. "I'm sure your mother waits every day for your return."

"Trust me, Mrs. Cox, it would not end well."

"Charles, we always wondered why you never returned home. Surely, your family rallied around you in support after your injuries," her father says.

I feel a tight constriction in my chest as I recall the day my brother came with my mother to visit me at the veteran's hospital. That long-anticipated reunion became a greater source of pain for me...

"With all due respect, I'd rather not talk about my family."

Candy looks upset, so I explain to them, "People like

to imagine discharged soldiers coming home to hometown parades and the loving arms of family and friends. It didn't happen that way for me and the many wounded servicemen I know. We came home to isolation and had to fight against the depression that followed. Not only were we scarred by the wounds we suffered in war but, on our return, we had to face the lack of understanding and support from those around us."

"I'm sorry to hear that," her mother says, her eyes filled with compassion.

I've buried the pain long ago and refuse to dig it back up. Changing the direction of the conversation, I look down at Candy and smile. "It's good to know at least one good thing came out of that town."

She blushes a pretty shade of pink.

"I still think you should go back, Charles," her father says. "We can make sure you get the hero's welcome you deserve."

I laugh sarcastically at the thought. After all these years, my return would only stir up bad feelings for everyone concerned. I tell him with all sincerity, "It's best to let sleeping dogs lie."

Her mom takes both my hands in hers, and I notice her hands no longer tremble. "Mr. Walker, I want you to know that I have no objections to you dating my daughter."

It's almost humorous—getting permission to date at my age. Especially from someone sixteen years my junior. But, there it is…

"Thank you, Mrs. Cox."

She surprises me by tentatively wrapping her arms around me in a hug. I'm shocked, but I dutifully return it.

These parents of Candy's are extraordinary people, much like their daughter.

Candy smiles as she watches me hug her mother, looking as if she knew all along that this is how it would play out. "I think it's high time we sat down to dinner, because this girl is starving!"

I choose to sit next to her father and am immediately bombarded with questions about Christmas movies. "Which one is your favorite of all time?"

I understand, based on what Candy has shared with me, that Christmas is a big deal for their family. However, I haven't celebrated the holiday since leaving the military, so I have to think about it, answering with the first one that comes to mind. "I'd say *How the Grinch Stole Christmas.*"

"The original or the Jim Carrey version?"

"I wasn't aware there was more than one version," I admit. "The cartoon came out when I was eight, so I naturally equate it with the holiday."

"It'll be interesting to see what you think of the newer version," her mother gushes. "We'll have to watch the original first, and then let you compare."

"Why would they redo a thirty-minute cartoon?" I ask, perplexed.

"The new one is a full-length movie, and it's hilarious," Candy assures me.

Her mother's eyes sparkle with excitement when she asks, "Oh, Charles, please tell me you've seen *Elf?*"

I'm totally out of my element here, and I glance in Candy's direction. The smile on her lips puts me at ease. Although the idea of Christmas died for me long ago, if it makes her happy and gives her parents a way to include me, who am I to resist?

"Do you have any favorite Christmas songs? We could put them on during dinner," her mother suggests.

I honestly haven't listened to one since I was a child. However, I distinctly remember what Candy was singing when we passed by each other in our cars. "I've always been partial to the song 'White Christmas'."

"Oh, my goodness, that's my favorite song of all time!" Candy squeals. "Do you like the movie, too?"

"There's a movie?"

Candy giggles.

"I'd have assumed you've seen it since it came out in 1954," her mother tells me.

"Hmm...that's a little before my time."

How old does she think I am? I wonder with amusement.

"As you can tell, Charles, our family really gets into Christmas," her father tells me before asking. "Do you feel it's something you can embrace?"

I wrap an arm around Candy's shoulder. "If this is something Candy enjoys, it's something I want to join her in."

Her father's heavy gaze rests on my arm around his daughter for a moment, and I realize I may have been too forward.

Just as I'm ready to remove my arm, he smiles. "A fine answer. I feel the same way about Katherine." He glances at his wife tenderly.

It appears I've been accepted by her parents—at least, initially. I hope never to break the trust they've placed in me concerning their daughter.

Her Acceptance

Candy

It's amazing how quickly my father's opinion of Captain changes once he makes the connection to Riley High. It's as if he sees Captain in a whole new light, even though he is the same man.

It means everything to me, because Dad now sees him the way I do.

Even my mother is beginning to see beyond his scars.

I have to stifle my laugh watching Captain, a no-nonsense man, decorating a gingerbread house with the precision of an engineer. My mother is relentless with him, making Captain join in every activity she has planned.

She's become like the Domme of Christmas or something.

Captain understands he is being tested and, to his credit, he not only endures it, but also excels in meeting her expectations without compromising his serious and sometimes stoic nature.

Being used to my father's naturally charismatic personality, Captain's stoic temperament takes a little getting used to for my mother. However, I find her over-the-top enthusiasm and his solemn disposition make for a unique dynamic that actually works.

Truly, having my parents treat Captain like part of our family has been the best Christmas gift I could have asked for and I'm actually sad when it's time for them to go.

"I wish you didn't have to leave," I whimper as my mom bends down to pick up her suitcase. Captain deftly sweeps in and takes it for her. "Allow me."

She smiles at him in gratitude, and then tells me, "Honestly, Cleo, I could celebrate Christmas all year long with you."

"You know I feel the same way," I agree enthusiastically. "Maybe we should plan for a short Christmas midway through the year."

My Mom turns to Captain. "What do you think, Charles?"

"I'd be willing, as long as there is plenty of Jack Daniels in the house..." He sees my mother's shocked expression and quickly adds, "For the hot chocolate, of course."

My dad chuckles, clapping him on the back. "I'll make sure to have a jug of it on hand."

Captain insists on driving my parents to the airport so the two of us can see them off.

"This was good," he tells me as we watch them make their way through security.

"It was the best," I agree. Wrapping my arm around his muscular arm, I rest my head against it. I haven't forgotten his promise to collar me. Temporary or not, I long to feel his collar around my neck.

"I have a special present for you, Captain," I mention. "I wanted to save it for when we were alone. Do you mind heading back to my place?"

"Not at all."

I have butterflies in my stomach on the ride back, wondering if he will like my unusual gift. It will either be utterly perfect or perfectly inappropriate.

When we enter my apartment, I ask him to sit on the couch while I fetch his gift. I return to him holding a small box in my hands. Rather than sit beside him, I choose to kneel at his feet.

"First, I would like to thank you for being so kind and accommodating to my parents. I know the whole Christmas thing isn't your style, but you made my mother happy and that always makes my father happy."

He chuckles. "Although I'll admit your mother can be overwhelming at times, her acceptance of me, along with your father's, was genuinely touching. I enjoyed my time with them."

"When my mom mentioned Christmas partway through the year and specifically asked you to join us, I have to be honest. I was floored."

He smirks. "Ah…well, I suppose I shouldn't have made that comment about needing Jack if that was the case."

"Oh, no. It was perfect. My dad totally appreciated it. Even he can't keep up with all of my mom's activities.

You were a real trouper."

"The fact that your parents trust me with their daughter is more than I have a right to ask. Humoring your mother is the least I can do."

I look down at the box in my hands, finally brave enough to present it to him. Holding it up to Captain, I smile nervously. "When I saw this, I felt it was meant for you. I hope you like it."

He takes the box from me. "No reason to be so anxious, pet. I'm sure I will like it." Captain slowly unwraps my gift and lifts the lid of the box, staring silently at the contents.

My heart races when he finally picks it up and states in a gruff voice, "An eye patch..."

"I like the sleek style. It fits your personality. Plus, it's made from premium leather with a strip on the inside made of breathable material. I was told it makes it more comfortable for long-term wear."

He studies it carefully, looking at it from all angles, feeling the edges of it with the pad of his thumb. Finally, he looks at me. "This is the last gift I would have expected from you."

"You don't like it," I say, wanting to get that out of the way so he doesn't have to pretend.

"Initially, I was put off, but only because I've worn this eye patch for years. It's become a part of me. This..." He looks at my gift again. "...this is like putting on a new appendage."

"I never thought of it that way. I'm sor—"

Captain puts his hand up to stop me. "Just because it isn't something I considered replacing, doesn't mean I don't appreciate your gift. Maybe it's time for a change."

I lick my lips nervously. "Would you let me put it on so you can see how it looks?"

He nods, handing me the eye patch.

My heart races as he reaches behind his head, untying his old patch and setting it down on the coffee table. I look up at him. His eye socket is sunken in, the upper and lower eyelids having melded together during the healing process. I know it isn't easy for him to expose himself to me like this.

And it makes me love him all the more…

I stand up and move in close, kissing Captain on the lips. "I love you." Gently placing the new patch over his eye socket, I tell him, "Adjust it until it feels comfortable and I'll secure it in the back."

Once he's satisfied with the fit, I reach around and tie it in place, drawing back to take a good look at him. The glossy, black leather eyepatch has stitching on the edges that gives it a sophisticated look. I can't help swooning as I stare at him. "Oh, Captain, you look so handsome."

"Do I?" he says, sounding amused.

I nod. "It suits you, but how does it feel?"

He moves his head around and makes different faces to get a feel for it. "It'll take some getting used to, but it actually seems a better fit than mine."

"Would you like me to get you a mirror so you can see for yourself?"

"No, pet. The fact that you like it is good enough for me."

My heart melts at his answer.

"I've brought something for you, as well."

I watch with bated breath as he pulls the thin black collar from his pocket. "Now that your parents are gone, it is time for you to wear this."

I know in my head that this is only a temporary collar, but my heart flutters as I kneel down before him to receive it. My skin tingles when I feel the leather collar press against my throat.

In a deep voice he vows, "This temporary collar symbolizes my commitment to protect you, my pet."

I close my eyes, my heart racing as he secures the buckle in the back. I love the pressure of it against my skin. It's like feeling his physical touch.

Opening my eyes, I make my own vow to him. "Captain, I accept your collar of protection, and will fully commit to each encounter you present to me."

He smiles, giving me a tender kiss on the cheek. "I will not fail you, my pet."

I remain convinced that he is my one, but I accept his conviction to the contrary, and I am willing to walk through this test with him.

"You make a beautiful sub," he says in a gravelly voice ripe with lust.

I touch the collar with my fingers, confessing, "Wearing this makes me feel more beautiful, Captain."

"You are always beautiful, my pet."

I lean toward Captain, wanting to thank him with a kiss. But, when our lips touch, I'm instantly hit by the sensual chemistry between us. He feels it too, and pulls me into him, kissing me more deeply.

My body responds to his sexual desire, drawn in by

his natural dominance. I run my hands through his hair, inadvertently loosening the eye patch because of my inadequate tie. It slips down and he instantly stiffens.

"Let me…" I purr.

Instead of retying it, I take it off completely.

It's a beautiful thing not to have that barrier between us, and I move in for another kiss.

At first, his lips are stiff and unyielding.

I know Captain feels vulnerable, being exposed like this, but when I lightly flick my tongue against his mouth, I'm gratified to hear the deep rumble of his passionate groan.

I open my lips slightly, inviting him in, and begin moaning softly as he explores my mouth with his tongue. Climbing onto his lap, I run my hands through his hair again, becoming completely lost in his kisses as he grasps the back of my neck and presses my lips firmly against his.

My Captain…

There is a sexual thrill to knowing the eye patch lays on the table beside us.

My pussy aches with need as he turns and slowly pushes me onto the couch. I look up at his beautiful, scarred face as he hurriedly unbuckles his belt and unzips his pants. The scars he carries are a part of who Captain is, heightening the intimacy between us. It makes this encounter far more personal than any before it.

My heart begins racing when I feel his hands hike up my skirt and slide off my wet panties. He caresses my body with his mouth and hands—his touch gentle, his kisses lingering.

I open my legs to him, needing to make love to this man. Arching my back, I moan as he pushes his cock into me—starting off with slow, measured strokes.

Reveling in the feeling of his hard shaft deep inside me, I wrap my legs around him, wanting even more. "I love you, Captain," I whisper, gazing up at him.

The look of love in his eyes makes me want to cry and I fight to hold back the tears.

Captain begins rolling his hips, taking me even more deeply, but with the same measured strokes, building up my desire as he stimulates my G-spot. However, my thoughts are not on my orgasm, but this intimate connection between us, and I don't want it to end.

But when he leans down and whispers in my ear as he comes, I am undone. Hearing Captain profess his love for me in this vulnerable moment takes me right over the edge and I climax, caressing his shaft with adoration.

He holds me for a long time afterward. It's as if, just like me, he doesn't want this connection to end.

Eventually, Captain releases the embrace and sits up, zipping up his pants and buckling his belt. He suddenly seems uncomfortable being openly exposed, and picks up the eye patch, turning away from me while he puts it on.

I'm secretly delighted he's chosen my gift over his old one.

Again, I'm struck by how handsome he looks in it. But, the truth is, Captain's just as handsome without it. It's my hope that someday he will come to a point when he no longer feels the need to wear it around me.

That would be the greatest compliment of all.

The Protector

Candy

C aptain asks me to dress up in a flirty little dress for my first encounter.

"Who am I dressing up for?" I ask, curious who his first Dom of choice is.

"Baron," he answers confidently. "I've seen the chemistry between you two. He is a fine protector, and a man who would treat you with the respect and care you deserve."

It's obvious that Captain has given great thought to this match.

As we drive to Baron's place, I start to feel my nerves kicking in.

"What's wrong, pet?"

"I'm not sure how I feel about this, Captain. I thought this would be like the scenes I did with the Doms during my Submissive Training classes, but it doesn't feel that way at all."

"I'm actually glad to hear you say that. It proves to

me that you are taking this challenge in the spirit it was designed. My mission is your happiness. Therefore, being true to yourself tonight, wherever it leads you, will guarantee you get the most out of this encounter."

I nod, still feeling anxious about it.

He reaches over and strokes my cheek. "If you leave tonight feeling differently toward Baron, I will be satisfied."

"And if I don't?"

"We will move on to the next Dom," he answers without hesitation. "The goal does not change."

Once we arrive at Baron's place, Captain helps me out of the car and walks me to the door. I sigh nervously, standing beside him as he knocks on the door.

Baron is quick to answer. "Captain and Candy, won't you please come in?"

Captain ushers me into the apartment, and I keep my gaze on the floor out of respect for Baron.

"No need for formalities tonight, Candy," Baron tells me. "I want to get to know you first. Eye contact is required this evening."

I gaze into his hazel eyes and smile. In a matter of seconds, Baron has already put me at ease.

"May I ask, Captain, how I received the honor of being the first chosen?" he asks as he leads us into the living room and gestures for us to sit.

"You were the obvious choice."

Baron glances at me and winks. "And how do *you* feel about the arrangement?"

I'm not sure how to answer, but end up telling him the truth, "I'm nervous."

Baron gives me a reassuring smile. "There's no need to be."

I glance around his apartment. Like Captain, he has simple tastes in furnishings, although he has an impressive entertainment system. I also notice pictures set about the room. They're all of the same woman. She's beautiful, with a confident smile and a stunning collar around her neck.

I've heard rumors that Baron lost his submissive in a mugging. Looking at her smiling face, I'm heartbroken that such a bright spirit is gone. Just like Ethan, her life ended far too soon.

"Since she is wearing your protection collar, would you like to go over your limits while she's in my care?"

"That won't be necessary," Captain says. "My desire is for you to interact naturally with her. The only limits will be any she voices herself."

I'm surprised by Captain's answer and glance at Baron, wondering what he has planned for me.

"It goes without saying that I will honor her limits," Baron replies. He looks at me while telling Captain, "Based on her experience with Liege, there is something specific I would like to focus on tonight."

"Good." Captain stands up. "Then I will take this opportunity to leave so you can begin."

"Don't leave just yet," Baron says. "I would like to ease Candy into this transition with your help."

"And how do you propose to do that?" he asks as he sits back down.

"I thought we'd start with a more personal conversation between the three of us."

Already, I am warming up to Baron's approach. He isn't overbearing, and I appreciate that he understands my unease.

"Candy, let me start by sharing something personal with you."

"Please."

"I see the same fire in you that I saw in my own Adrianna. She was stubborn like you, with the same fierce loyalty. Sir Davis introduced us at her graduation ceremony. I'll never forget that moment. My life stopped and became something new when I met Adrianna for the first time. I was completely and utterly taken with that woman."

His full lips spread into a mesmerizing smile as he talks about her. "Adrianna had a dynamic personality that both comforted and challenged me. That woman carried herself with a confidence that a lesser man might mistake as arrogance, but she was anything but. No, she was a calm female presence wrapped around an intensely sharp mind.

"My baby was the kind of woman that instinctually made you want to meet her high standards. And you can bet she had a harem of men vying for her attention when I met her."

Baron smiles at me with those striking hazel eyes, confessing, "I believe Sir Davis knew exactly what would happen when he introduced the two of us."

Baron sits back against the couch, chuckling lightly. "I knew as soon as we met that she was the one. It was like meeting a missing part of my soul. When Adrianna agreed to be mine, her submission was unconditional, and I have yet to experience that level of power exchange again."

Seeing the love in Baron's eyes made my heart ache for him. I look at her pictures around the room and tell him, "But she's with you."

He smiles. "Yes, she's always with me."

I glance at Captain. "It's strange that all three of us carry someone with us from our past."

He nods, a troubled look in his eye.

I still don't know who Grapes is, but I know the man had a huge impact on Captain's life. I decide now is a good time to find out more about him. But, rather than ask Captain about it directly, I turn to Baron. "I have only heard the barest of details about her death. Do you mind telling me what happened?"

I see the question pains him, and I instantly feel a deeper connection with Baron, since I feel the same way about Ethan's death.

Baron glances at the nearest picture of her. "It was a simple night out. A late-night movie at our favorite theater. When we came out after the show, it was raining heavily. I went to get the car to spare her from getting drenched." He pauses for a moment, his eyes clouded with sorrow. "When I pulled up to the theater entrance, I found her on the pavement, bloody and unresponsive, nobody else in sight. I later found out she had been attacked by three juveniles for the forty dollars she had in her purse…"

He growls under his breath, but soon that haunted look returns as his gaze darts back to her picture. "I rushed her straight to the hospital, but my baby never regained consciousness…"

Tears run down my face as I share in his pain.

Baron continues, "I'm haunted by the fact I never had the chance to tell her I loved her one last time, or to tell her I was sorry."

I close my eyes, trying not to sob. His regret matches my own.

"I understand," Captain states in a gravelly voice full of emotion.

I look over to see he is crying. My heart is crushed, and I want to rush over to comfort him, but I stay still. I'm afraid any movement on my part might disturb this rare moment of openness.

"The guilt you carry when you feel responsible for their deaths is the most damaging emotional of all," he says, wiping the tears from his good eye.

"It is," Baron agrees.

"As a Captain, you know your men's lives are on the line anytime you're on the battlefield—it's a burden you always carry. But nothing prepared me for that day…"

He swallows hard several times and then looks at me. The depth of pain I see in his face overshadows my own, and I struggle to breathe for a moment.

"Grapes was the very first casualty. We never saw it coming. One moment he's standing beside me, and the next, he's…gone."

Captain glances over at Baron. "I agree that it's the things you didn't get a chance to say that end up tormenting you." He shakes his head, a look of anguish on his face. "He and I had a tendency to give each other grief. That's how we communicated. But Grapes was the best friend that I've ever had." Captain looks at me with regret. "I never told him how much I admired him as a person. Adam never knew how truly exceptional he was." His voice starts to choke up and he turns away from me.

In this short exchange, Captain has given me the information I have longed for. Grapes was his best friend, he died the day Captain lost all of his men, and his first name was Adam.

"How have you dealt with the guilt?" Baron asks him.

Captain gives a sarcastic snort. "Not very well, obviously."

Baron turns his attention back on me. "Like you, I've only heard bits and pieces from others. What happened to Ethan?"

My heart stops for a moment as the sounds of crunching metal and shattering glass ring in my head. It takes me a few moments to settle the emotions it evokes before I can speak.

"Like you, it was a simple outing. I suggested we go for ice cream and wanted to walk since it was close by..." My throat closes up as the pain takes over.

"It's okay, pet," Captain encourages me.

I nod, grateful for his presence. "We were crossing the street when a big white truck came barreling straight at us. I froze, but Ethan pushed me out of the way before impact." I cover my face and start crying.

I feel Captain's hand as he rubs my back gently in silent support.

"Ethan died saving me and, like both of you, it was

as if one moment he was there, and the next he was gone. I still can't wrap my head around it." I can't stop the tears from falling as I share. "The worst part is that I never got the chance to say goodbye or to thank him."

Baron nods while Captain wraps his strong arms around me.

"Let's face it. A sudden death leaves a wound that's nearly impossible to heal," Baron says. "It's been years, and I'm still blindsided by the loss. Every time I think I've made headway, I catch her scent or see her favorite flower and I'm completely undone. The hardest thing for me is that it hurts just as much now as it did when I found her on the sidewalk."

I swallow down the lump in my throat. "I know...I feel that way about Ethan. It just takes seeing a big white truck and I break down in tears. I keep retracing my steps, wishing to God I had taken Ethan up on his offer to drive me instead of walking. If I'd just said yes, none of this would have happened and he would still be alive."

"I completely understand feeling that way," Baron says. "If I hadn't left Adrianna to get the car, she would not have been alone when those boys showed up..." His voice trails off as he's hit anew with grief.

We are both locked in a single point in time, and neither of us we can free ourselves from it.

"It's been twenty-six years, and I have to say that the pain never goes away. You simply learn to live with it," Captain tells us. "As far as the guilt, you need to let it go. What happened was pure chance in both your cases. It wasn't a mistake on either of your parts that resulted in their deaths. Holding onto that guilt is pointless and damaging. It helps no one."

"I know you are right," Baron replies, "but that is easier said than done."

"Yes," I agree. "I'm helpless to stop replaying what happened no matter how hard I try."

Captain looks at me seriously. "You must find a way, pet. You are only hurting yourself and doing Ethan no service."

"I will say that something good has come from the guilt, though," Baron interjects. "I have found great satisfaction in my mission of rescuing new submissives from abusive Dom wannabes."

"Yes, and that is something I greatly admire about you," Captain tells him.

"The one good thing to come out of Ethan's death was that it eventually led me to you, Captain."

He shakes his head. "No, the future holds so much more for you, my pet."

"And on that note, I think we transition to the next phase of the evening," Baron announces. "After a little heart to heart session, it's always good to follow it up with a kiss." He stands up and walks over to the couch, sitting on the other side of me.

"Give your Master a kiss," he commands in a low, seductive voice.

I turn my head toward Captain and lean forward. Giving him a gentle kiss on the lips, my emotions still raw from our conversation. It starts out almost tentativly, both of us having exposed so much of ourselves in the conversation but, as his kiss continues, it becomes more passionate and intense.

Captain brushes away the remaining tears on my cheeks and kisses me more deeply. By the time he releases me from his embrace, I am wet with desire.

"Very nice," Baron compliments, in his silky smooth baritone. "Now kiss me."

I automatically glance at Captain, who nods his approval. With my heart beating rapidly, I lean up and kiss Baron's full lips. He groans in response, pulling me into his kiss. The chemistry we felt at the graduation ceremony is enhanced by the emotional connection we now share. I get lost in his passionate kiss and the spicy taste of his lips.

When I finally pull back, I feel a little light-headed.

Captain commands, "Kiss me again while Baron touches you."

I almost feel faint when our lips meet again and I feel Baron's hand run lightly over the material of my dress, his touch light as he caresses my shoulder before heading to my nipple and down my stomach and then even lower…teasing me with his light touches.

Captain seems to enjoy this new dynamic, his kisses becoming even more fervent than before. I sense no jealousy coming from him, and I give in to their dual attention.

I stiffen, however, when I feel Baron's hand sneak underneath my panties.

"Relax," Captain whispers as he slips his fingers under my panties, as well. I instinctively spread my legs wider, inviting both men to continue.

Soon, I am moaning in pure pleasure, my pussy aching as it builds toward climax while I alternate kisses from one man to the other.

It is pure decadence to have these two men pleasing my body at the same time, and I give in fully to the experience, crying out in pleasure when Baron tells me to come. I hold my breath as my orgasm reaches its zenith, extremely turned on by having both men play with me.

My back arches of its own accord as my body finds release in a beautiful crescendo of sensual pulses, each one taking my breath away in its intensity.

I lay there afterward, repeating to myself, "Wow...just wow."

Captain stares at me tenderly. "You are beautiful when you climax."

"Agreed," Baron answers, kissing my wet mound in appreciation before kissing me on the lips.

I am such a spoiled sub...

"This is where I leave," Captain states, standing up stiffly, his erection outlined in his pants.

"Let me relieve you of this," I tell him playfully, looking at his hard cock trapped in the tight material.

"I'm fine," he insists, holding out his hand to Baron.

Baron stands to shake his hand but he, too, is sporting an impression erection. I feel both proud and humbled. Proud that I have had that effect on them, and humbled that they chose to please me and not themselves.

"Let me see you out," Baron insists.

Captain turns to me, "Stay here, pet. There is something I need to discuss with Baron."

I nod my consent and dutifully stay behind, but the nerves from before suddenly kick in again as they talk quietly at the door. After Captain leaves, Baron returns and sits beside me on the couch.

"I told you there was something I would like to focus on tonight."

I nod, my heart racing because I know it has something to do with Liege.

"You once shared that Liege hurt you while having anal sex."

My eyes widen. That experience is something I never want to repeat, and it's not a scene I would willingly choose.

"I see by your expression the damage he has done." Baron strokes my cheek tenderly. "Anal sex can be quite sensual and pleasing for both partners. I want to return that to you."

I can't hide my fear, but ask, "How?"

"The two of us would enjoy some extensive foreplay to ready your body and mind, I would apply plenty of lube, and we'd start with this." He reaches into his pocket and pulls out a jeweled butt plug. "As you can see, this one is small and will go in easily."

He hands it to me. I'm charmed by the pretty gold and pink jewel. Baron is right, it isn't big enough to be intimidating.

"Once your body is primed with this, you will be ready to begin, and I promise to take it as slow as you need. My primary goal is to bring you pleasure tonight."

I frown. "But isn't that my job as a sub?"

"It is, and tonight your pleasure is my pleasure."

I let out a nervous sigh. Although I trust Baron, this is a hard limit for me because of my experience with

Liege. "What happens if, despite all you've done, it still hurts?"

"Then we stop. The last thing I want to do is hurt you."

I nod my head calmly, but there are conflicting emotions running through me. I know the decision lies with me. Although it scares me, I also know this is something Captain would never challenge me with. He likes to spoil me, not test me.

I could walk away from this offer and never have to face it again. Or…I could trust Baron and possibly erase that memory of Liege forever. The idea of that proves too great and I agree.

Baron kisses me on the lips, his eyes flashing with excitement. "To be the one to change your experience is an honor, Candy."

The fact that Baron cares so deeply about this only heightens my confidence in him as my Dom. Knowing my safeword is my way out, I eagerly comply when he tells me to undress.

"You are a cute little thing," he says as he picks me up in his arms and carries me to his bedroom.

Laying me on his bed, he tells me with a smirk, "Foreplay begins with eye candy, Candy."

I giggle, watching as he unbuttons his shirt and pulls it back, exposing his dark skin and those toned chest and stomach muscles. I very much appreciate his eye candy.

Baron then unbuckles his pants, pulling his belt out of the belt loops and letting it fall to the floor. The sound of the metal buckle hitting the floor sends a pleasant shiver through my whole body. Slowly unzipping his jeans, Baron pulls them down, along with his boxers.

His erection is quite impressive, but the look in his eyes has me totally captivated.

Once fully undressed, he comes back to the bed and lies beside me. "Let me tastes those lips again."

I melt into Baron's embrace, swept away by his comfortable dominance. His kisses excite me and his hands tease me until I'm trembling with desire.

That's when he orders me to sit on his face while I suck his cock. I purr in delight but, because of my small size, it's a challenge for us. With my pussy positioned over his mouth, I can only reach the head of his cock with my lips, and I have to stroke the rest of his shaft with my hand.

Baron doesn't seem to mind, going down on my pussy as he orders me to please him. The stimulation of being eaten while sucking his cock sends jolts of electricity through my body. I never knew how sexy sixty-nining could be, but my enthusiasm proves too much and he orders me to stop several times.

The third time, he gives up and rolls me onto the bed beside him, chuckling as he looks at me. "There's only so much a man can take."

I grin. "But it's so much fun, I don't want to stop yet."

"We can start up again, but we must do something first."

Baron leaves the bed for a moment and returns with a bottle of lube and the pretty butt plug. I stare at it warily as he covers it in lubricant.

"No need to fear it," he assures me. Baron orders me on all fours before rejoining me on the bed. I bite my lip when I feel his hand, slick with lubricant, caressing the rim of my ass. It suddenly becomes real for me and I start breathing fast. I have to block out the memories of Liege. This experience is not the same, and I want to know what Baron can teach me.

"Relax. You'll like this," he assures me in that sexy baritone.

After he has thoroughly coated my ass with lubricant, he places the cold metal of the butt plug against it. "I'll only press lightly. It will be your body that invites it in," he tells me. "All I need you to do is bear down."

I close my eyes as I push with my inner muscles, and the most amazing thing happens. The toy slips inside with no pain whatsoever. I look back at him in surprise.

He just smiles and asks, "How does it feel?"

The sensations are so new, I have to think for a moment before I answer. "It feels good, but strange. I like the feeling of fullness."

"And your ass is that much more adorable with that jewel," he compliments, as he wipes his hands off with a hand towel. "Are you ready to sixty-nine me again?"

I am eager to, and feel a little kinkier with the toy inside me.

I climb back into position and grasp his thick cock. This time, however, I lick the head of it like a kitten—with light, but rapid, strokes of my tongue.

"Oh, hell…what are you doing? It feels too fucking good!"

I take that as permission to continue and return my

attention to his cock. Baron groans loudly before pressing my pussy against his mouth and teaching me the mastery of his tongue.

I feel the tension building to dizzying heights, and I momentarily stop as it overtakes me and I come against his tongue, the toy lodged in my ass. I find it exciting and mew softly afterward, overwhelmed by the intensity of my orgasm.

I grasp his cock again and stick out my tongue to catch the precum glistening on the head of his shaft.

"Not another lick," he orders.

Before I can protest, Baron lifts me off himself. He stares down at his raging hard-on and tells me, "I'm ready if you're willing."

My pussy contracts in pleasure and fear. I remember the pain when Liege did it, but nothing I've experienced with Baron is remotely similar and I'm aching for more.

In answer, I get on all fours and look back at him.

Baron's hazel eyes glint with desire as he positions himself behind me. "You'll need to relax as I pull the plug out."

I close my eyes as I concentrate on relaxing. For some unexplainable reason, my body resists the toy leaving, and I have to focus on relaxing my muscles enough to let go.

Baron immediately replaces the toy with his lubricated fingers, stroking the inside of my ass to further lubricate and prepare me for his cock. My whole body is tingling in excitement and anticipation, but the fear lingers.

"Do you want to call your safeword?" he asks.

It is in this moment when I fully submit to Baron, trusting him enough to cross my hard limit.

"No, I want you to take me."

I wait, my breath coming in short, quick gaps as he lubricates his shaft before positioning himself behind me.

Baron places one hand on my right butt cheek to help guide me and says, "Rock against me gently so your body can adjust. You are in control. I will not move."

Being in control at this moment is exactly what I need to hear, and I turn to look back at him as I begin to rock, the head of his cock pressing against my sensitive hole.

Because of the butt plug, my muscles are less tight, and I find it's not painful as I take more of the head of his shaft. Remembering the trick with the toy, I bear down and am surprised when the entire head slips inside. I freeze for a moment, shocked by the fullness of his cock inside my ass, but Baron is right, I feel no pain.

When I feel I'm ready to continue, I begin rocking against him again, taking more and more of his cock.

"It's sexy to watch my dark shaft disappear into that tight ass," he comments.

His words turn me on, making me even wetter. I keep up the motion, stopping from time to time to let my body adjust. True to his word, Baron never moves, letting me decide on the depth and pressure.

There comes a point when his hard shaft is deep inside my ass that I choose to give up control. I look back and gaze into those hazel eyes. "Take me, Baron."

He lets out a manly growl of satisfaction as he grabs

my buttocks and slowly pulls out. My body resists his leaving, squeezing his cock tightly in protest. He them pushes back inside, centimeter by centimeter. All the nerve endings in my ass fire off at once, making me shiver in delight.

Baron lowers himself, wrapping one arm under my stomach in an intimate embrace as he begins rolling his hips—each stroke slow and sensual.

I am completely under his erotic spell. I purr in pleasure, delighting in this kinky but intimate exchange.

Baron's claiming is slow and gentle. When he finally orgasms, I join his cry of passion as he coats my ass with his come.

Afterward, as we lay together I can't stop smiling.

"What?" he asks in amusement.

"I never thought it could be like that, Baron."

He kisses me on the forehead. "Now you know."

I look at him in wonder. "You're amazing."

He chuckles. "I certainly don't mind hearing that after a scene…"

"No, Baron. I'm serious. I don't know how I can ever thank you."

"Enjoy a good session of anal sex every now and then. That will be thanks enough."

When Captain returns to take me home, I see his expression is one of concern as soon as he walks through the door. "Everything went well?" he asks.

"Very well, Captain."

His smile is genuine when he replies, "I'm glad to hear it, pet."

Captain holds out his hand to Baron. "Thank you. I

can see by the look on her face that you had a successful evening."

"It went better than I hoped."

Captain looks back at me. "I look forward to hearing all about it."

I smile. What he doesn't know yet is that tonight has not only provided me with healing, but clarity as well.

Trouper

Captain

I leave Baron's, trusting him with Candy tonight. It's not easy for me, knowing what Baron plans to do.

Candy carries emotional scars caused by Liege's abuse, and while I can see Baron's point about addressing this one in particular, it may prove too much for her.

I look back at his apartment.

I have to trust that Candy will use her safeword, if needed, and that Baron will know if things have gone too far if she does not.

I let out an uneasy sigh as I start my vehicle. Rather than return home to dwell on it, I head to the pet shop where Candy and I met for our first scene together. I have fond memories of our encounter and prefer to think back on that, instead.

Like Candy, I enjoy watching young animals play. Their innocence and boundless energy can provide countless hours of entertainment.

I notice an Australian Shepherd pup with the characteristic one blue eye and one brown. It reminds me of Trouper. I credit that dog for saving my life at a time when I had lost all hope.

After recovering from my injuries enough to be discharged from the veteran's hospital, I went down a dark path. I had no friends, no family, and no reason to live other than the debt I owed to my men who died that day.

I became a hermit, living off the money I'd saved during my service, only leaving the apartment at night for food and supplies. The lack of human contact began to have a negative effect on me as I sank into a deep depression.

Plagued by memories of the battle, I relived it day after day, wishing I had been more aware, more cautious, more *anything* that could have saved my men. I was drowning in the guilt I carried, and even the desire to honor the lives of my men was no longer enough to make it through each day.

That's when Trouper entered my life in the most horrifying way.

The terrified shrieking won't stop. I can't make it stop.

I shake my head, trying to force the sound out of my mind. It takes a few moments for me to realize the sound is coming from outside my apartment.

It's the desperate cry of a wounded animal. The shrillness and terror in its shrieks pull at my heart, and

I'm driven to find this poor animal and put it out of its misery.

I race outside to find a crowd of women and children gathered beside the busy road. A dog lies in the middle of the street, surrounded by a pool of blood.

The poor animal is nearly hit again as cars swerve around it, trying to avoid the creature. I run into the street, holding my hand up to stop the traffic.

I call out to the dog as I approach, trying to reassure the wounded animal that I am here to help. As I draw nearer, I see it's an Australian Shepherd and its teeth are bared. One of the dog's hind legs has been crushed and is bleeding profusely. I know I have to act fast or the animal will die right here in the road.

However, the animal is in extreme pain and growls ominously as I get closer.

"I'm here to help," I tell him in a calm voice. "You can bite me, but it's only going to hinder your rescue, pup."

I look to confirm all the traffic has stopped before kneeling down beside the dog. I explain to him what I'm doing, just as I used to with my wounded men. I keep my tone soothing and steady as I speak, wanting the dog to know my intention is to help, not harm.

I slowly lay my hand on his shoulder as he continues to growl at me, but the dog does not try to bite me. Slipping my arms under him, I try to lift him. But the moment I lift him off the ground, he begins shrieking again.

"I know it hurts, buddy, but you need to be brave…"

Picking up a wounded animal is a risk, but I can't

leave him in the road. Gritting my teeth, I lift the shrieking dog and carry him off the road and over to a soft patch of grass. I gently set him down, praising him for not taking a chunk out of me.

Knowing I have to stop the bleeding, I rip off my shirt and fashion a makeshift tourniquet around his hind leg.

The crowd gathers around me to watch, and one of the women speaks up. "It happened in front of the house while the kids were playing. Some boy in a Jeep came racing down the road. He didn't even stop when he hit the dog. He just kept going. What if it had been a child?"

The other women in the crowd mumble their concern, but instantly turn silent when the dog yelps in pain.

"There's so much blood..." the woman murmurs.

A little boy asks me, "Is he going to be okay, mister?"

I look up to assure him, saying, "I'll do everything I can."

He stares at me with his mouth wide open, gawking at the scars that cover half of my face and chest. I see that glimmer of fear in his eyes as he backs away from me, running to hide behind his mother.

I'm suddenly aware that *everyone* is staring at me.

I ignore them, concentrating my efforts on the dog, instead. "Easy, boy. You're going to be okay."

"Is this your dog?" another woman asks, breaking the uneasy silence that has fallen over the crowd.

"No, I don't have any pets."

Since the animal is not wearing a collar, I ask the

group, "Does anyone know who owns this dog?"

An older girl avoids looking at me, but answers. "I think it's a stray. I've seen it running around the last couple of weeks."

The animal's dirty coat, along with the calloused pads of its feet, corroborates her story. The poor animal must be a long way from home.

"I'm going to get my car," I tell the adults. "Keep an eye on him."

I race to my apartment and throw on a t-shirt before ripping the comforter from my bed. I pull my car up to the sidewalk beside him and find the group has grown in that short amount of time.

They make way for me as I head back to get the dog. The poor creature is whining piteously, leaving me to wonder if he will survive the trip.

As gently as I can, I work the blanket under him, then ask the group, "I need one of you to grab the other end and help me lift him so we can slide him into the car."

No one moves to help.

I'm about to assign the job to somebody when one of the women finally volunteers. I grab the end near the animal's mouth, not wanting to risk her being bitten during transport.

The injured dog growls and begins yelping in pain as we carry him to the vehicle and slide him into the backseat. I shut the door and nod to the woman in thanks before jumping into the driver's seat.

She knocks on the passenger side window and says through the glass, "I can go with you."

Concerned for the dog's survival, I roll down the window and agree, telling her, "Why don't you drive and I'll stay in the back to keep the dog still."

She nods and turns to her kids, "Stay with Ms. Julie until I get back."

"Please save him, Mommy!" the little boy cries.

"We'll do our best, honey."

The trip to the clinic proves exceedingly painful for the poor dog, and I suffer several minor bites trying to keep him still as we drive over the bumps. However, I know the dog is doing its best to control the urge to bite every time we hit another bump.

Once we arrive at the vet hospital, one of the assistants runs out to help us. "We got a call from your neighbors letting us know you were coming."

With his help, we get the dog inside, and they take him straight to the operating room while I'm left to fill out forms.

"Are you the owner?" the receptionist asks.

"No, we believe the dog is a stray."

"Are you willing to take financial responsibility for this dog if the owner cannot be located?"

"Yes," I answer, even though I have no desire to own a pet.

"After the vet makes her initial assessment, she'll discuss treatment options and the costs associated with each one."

I nod to her.

Once I'm done with the stack of forms, I turn to the woman who accompanied me and ask, "Would you like me to drive you home?"

"No. If you don't mind, I'd rather stay and find out if the dog is going to make it."

I shrug. "It's fine with me, but I have no idea how long this will take, and you have children to look after."

"Don't worry about my brood. Julie's great, and my kids are best friends with hers."

"Take a seat, then. This may take a while."

The vet comes out twenty minutes later and motions for me to join her in the operating room. The Australian Shepherd lays on the table, its tongue lolling out and its eyes half-open.

"I've managed to stop the bleeding, Mr. Walker, and have sedated the dog. I was told you're taking responsibility for him, so the decision is yours on how I should proceed. We have two options. I can either remove the leg or I can euthanize him. Obviously, if I remove the leg, there is a considerable expense involved, but I am willing to lower the cost because of the circumstances. However, it means you will need to care for the dog until he recovers, and you should be aware that dogs with a missing limb have a harder time being adopted."

I stare at the dog, saying nothing as I weigh the two options. Euthanasia will put the animal out of its misery. However, I've lost too many of my own men, and the idea of killing this innocent creature makes my skin crawl.

I don't need a dog. I don't want a dog. However, I can't walk away.

"Remove the leg."

The vet smiles. "I'll call you back in after the procedure."

I return to the waiting room and Alice greets me with an anxious look. "So?"

"They are removing the leg. The dog should be fine."

"Oh, thank goodness!"

"I don't suppose you want a dog?" I ask hopefully.

"Oh, no! I have enough to handle with my brood."

I sit back down, realizing I've just become a new owner. I shake my head, thinking what a fine pair we make—One-Eye and His Three-Legged Mutt.

Life sure has a perverse sense of humor.

I bring the dog home two days later with a long list of instructions on how to care for him. He doesn't look to be doing well and lies listlessly in the dog bed I purchased.

Every now and then, he whimpers.

Like clockwork, I redress his wounds at the appointed time, and try to get food down him as often as I can but each day, he seems to worsen. When I can't take the sound of his whimpering any longer, I bring him to my bed.

Lying beside him, I pet the dog. With tears running down my face, I tell him, "Be a trouper, pup. Don't give up on me." The dog wags his tail once in response. I don't even know this damn animal, but I seriously can't bear the thought of him dying.

To ensure his recovery, I stop feeding him the

canned dog food and start feeding him real meat. It doesn't take long before I start seeing an improvement, but I've created a problem with my constant care.

The dang animal doesn't want me to leave his side, and he must rest to heal from the major surgery he's had. However, when I leave the room, he tries to follow me. If I shut him away in the room, he howls. Even if I barricade the doorway so he can still see me, he howls.

Eventually, I decide he's rested enough and set him free.

He hops toward me, his tail wagging vigorously. Laying his head on my lap, he looks up at me with his blue and brown eyes.

"What do you want?"

He just wags his tail, waiting.

Waiting for what, I have no idea. I pat him on the head. "Are you hungry? Is that what you want?"

His eyes never leave me. I finally get up and dish up some meat for him, setting it on the floor. He sniffs at it, disinterested, then looks up at me again with an expectant look.

"You're going to drive me crazy, dog."

I go back to the couch and sit down, amused when he returns, laying his head on my lap, that expectant look returning while his tail wags slowly.

After trying everything I can think of, I finally spy the leash. As soon as I grab it, he starts barking excitedly. Even though I despise going out in public, there's no stopping this dog from having a walk.

I sigh as I clip the leash to his collar and head out for a short walk around the block. As soon as the kids see him, they run over and start peppering me with questions.

"Is he's okay now?"

"Can we pet him?"

"What's his name?"

A name...

I haven't gotten that far yet but, as I look down at him balancing on his three legs, it comes to me. "Trouper. Troup for short."

"Aww..." one of the girls says, kneeling down and rubbing his furry cheeks. "You're so cute, Trouper."

I'm amazed as the kids gather around me to pet the dog. Having Troup seems to have made them forget all about my monstrous face.

When I feel the dog has had enough of their attention, I announce that I am taking him for a walk. While I had originally planned to take a short walk around the block, I end up walking several more because Troup doesn't want to stop.

His zest for life is contagious.

When we finally return to the apartment, I find a basket waiting for me on the doorstep. I pick up the basket and take it inside, curious about who sent it. Inside, I find a batch of homemade peanut butter cookies and a note.

Mr. Walker,

I wanted to personally thank you for saving that sweet dog. I can't tell you how happy all the kids in the neighborhood were when Alice told us the dog was going to live because of you.

You made what could have been a traumatic experience for our children into an example of how kind and generous people can be.

Thank you, Mr. Walker, and God bless you!
One Grateful Mother

I immediately sit down after reading the note, overcome with emotion. I put my head in my hands and start to cry. Troup immediately sticks his nose between my hands in concern.

My sudden outburst of emotion is a shock to me, but after months of feeling utterly alone and invisible, the neighbor who sent me these cookies cannot know what her act of kindness means.

I take one of the cookies from the basket and break it in half, handing one piece to Trouper. "You've earned it, buddy."

As he gobbles it up, I take a bite of the cookie myself and sigh.

With that one bite, I have entered the land of the living again…

I give the little Australian pup a scratch on the head and thank the owner of the pet store before I leave.

Baron set a time for me to return for Candy, and I

haven't received a text requesting more time so I return, assuming everything has gone well. However, I can't be sure of that until I see Candy in person.

When I walk through his door, I can immediately tell by the expression on her face that this has been a successful evening. The bright glint in her eyes makes me wonder if it might have been even more than that.

After sharing pleasantries with Baron, I escort Candy to my car.

On the drive home, she can't stop talking about how incredible the night was and how surprised she is to find she actually enjoys anal sex. She surprises me by asking, "Is that something you would ever consider doing with me, Captain?"

My cock stirs at the suggestion, but I answer nonchalantly, "If it would please you, pet."

"I would definitely like to try it with you. I never knew how intimate it could be."

"I must say I'm surprised at your enthusiasm, knowing it is one of your hard limits."

She blushes. "To be honest, I am, too. But Baron showed me what's possible, and I feel like I've missed out on something wonderful."

"You have your whole life ahead to make up for it."

Candy reaches over and places her hand on my thigh. "Yes, I do!"

"What are your feelings for Baron now?"

She bats her eyes at me, her smile growing wider. "Baron is an amazing Dom and person. Like you, he has an easy dominance that fits my personality well. You were right to pick him as my first."

Her answer prompts me to ask the next question. "Does that mean your feelings have changed?"

"It does. I absolutely admire him, and I hope to get to know him better."

"So, our search has ended?" I press.

She looks at me and smiles as she shakes her head.

I know I shouldn't feel as relieved as I do but the truth is, I'm not quite ready to let her go yet.

"So, we move on to my second choice?" I ask.

"If it pleases you." She sits back in her seat with a satisfied grin. "I thank you for tonight, Captain. This evening was more than I could have hoped for."

"That pleases me more than I can say, pet."

With the memories still fresh in my mind after my visit to the pet shop, I ask, "What would you think if I told you I wanted a dog?"

The Mystery

Candy

Captain instructs me to wear an elegant but simple black dress. He seems uncharacteristically excited for me to scene with this next Dom but he won't give me a name, only hints about who he is.

"The man is not only and accomplished Dom, but he is an astute businessman, as well," Captain informs me. "Talking to him, I was immediately impressed by his sharp mind."

"But why all the secrecy, Captain?" I ask, amused to see him so animated.

"This person isn't someone you would consider for yourself, but I suspect you two are a good match. More importantly, he's someone I trust to treat you with the respect and compassion you deserve."

When I hear him talk about these other Doms, I'm continually struck by the fact that the characteristics he looks for in these other men are the very ones he himself possesses. I understand that Captain needs to come to that conclusion himself, and I am okay with that because wearing his collar—temporary or not—means I get to spend more time with him.

Captain's hints make me even more curious about the Dom I will be scening with tonight, so I ask, "Is he someone I know?"

"Affirmative."

"Is that the extent of your answer?"

He smirks. "I'm looking forward to seeing the look on your face when you see who it is."

I shake my head, but I have to admit I like seeing this playful side of Captain.

He drives us through an older neighborhood before pulling up to an historical Victorian home. "Are you ready for this?"

I look at the house, curious about who owns it. "I am, but I'm also a little nervous. You said I would never choose him, so what if it turns out we aren't a match? Like—at all?"

"Then I want you to use your safeword and call me. I'll come back for you immediately." He caresses my cheek. "Based on your experience with Baron, however, I'm confident this will be a positive experience for you."

I trust Captain, but still...

He can see the concern in my eyes and adds, "I will say this—the man is familiar with your temperament and needs. No matter what he has planned tonight, you'll be determining the course of the evening."

I instantly feel more at ease and gratefully take his hand as he helps me out of the car.

As we make our way up to the door, he asks, "Who

do you think it is, my pet?"

"At first, I was convinced it was Dominare, the last Dom I had asked to interview the day of my graduation. However, you mentioned this is a Dom I wouldn't pick, so I immediately ruled him out. Then I thought it might be Rytsar Durov, and I was terrified. But I know you would never pair me with a sadist." As I look up at the ornate wooden decorations covering the outside of Victorian-style house, I admit, "So I settled on Tono Nosaka, but this does not look like his style at all."

I smile at Captain, shrugging. "I'm at a loss. Honestly, I have no idea who will answer this door."

"Perfect." Captain rings the doorbell and stands back, watching me intently.

My heart begins to race when I hear footsteps coming toward the door, and I stop breathing when it swings open.

"Well, howdy, Miss Cox What brings you out to my neck of the woods?" he asks with a charming smile.

Master Anderson…

Captain is right. He wasn't even on my radar, and my jaw drops. The cowboy Dom is an expert with the bullwhip, which is not a tool I even want to try.

I look at Captain questioningly.

Master Anderson holds out his hand to Captain. "Good to see you again."

"Likewise."

"I see your submissive is properly surprised."

Captain has a glint in his eye. "It was the exact reaction I was counting on."

"Please come in, both of you," Master Anderson tells

us.

As we walk through the hallway, I find all the decorative architecture throughout his home enchanting. "This place is amazing, Master Anderson."

"Thank you. It's not quite what I had in Denver, but it still maintains the same charm."

We sit down in a living room, and Master Anderson asks, "Tell me, Miss Cox. What are your thoughts about this pairing?"

"I admit I'm...surprised."

"I was too when Captain first explained his proposal, yet...he's right. I do like itty-bitty things with the hearts of a lion."

I blush, remembering his compliment the night of my graduation.

Captain speaks up. "I thought the levity you bring would match well with Candy's carefree spirit."

"Do you like a good practical joke, darlin'?" Master Anderson asks.

"Well, I do like them... but more when they're played on someone else."

He chuckles. "It's much more fun, I agree."

As I stare at Master Anderson, I realized this can't possibly work, based on the rules of the Submissive Training Center.

I address Captain in concern. "I have a question."

"Yes?"

"Since Master Anderson was my trainer, doesn't that preclude him collaring me?"

Captain nods to Master Anderson proudly. "I told you she's a smart one." He then looks at me and smiles tenderly. "I specifically discussed the matter with Master Anderson, but I will let him share his thoughts with you later."

Standing up, Captain walks over to Master Anderson. "Call me if you require extra time."

Master Anderson glances at me and winks. "Will do."

Holding out his arms, Captain calls me to him. I walk over, closing my eyes as I lay my head on his chest.

"Embrace this unique opportunity, my pet," he whispers.

I nod, not quite ready for him to go.

"Kneel," Captain commands.

I immediately kneel on the floor and look up at him.

Since Master Anderson is one of my official trainers, Captain places his hand on my head, and states, "I give my ownership of you over to Master Anderson. Serve him well tonight, my pet."

He lifts his hand and tells me to remain still.

I feel Master Anderson place his hand on my head. "I accept your submission, slave. You will call me Master for the remainder of the night."

I feel butterflies in my stomach on hearing his command. This will be a formal power exchange, not the casual one I experienced with Baron.

Keeping my head down, I answer, "Yes, Master."

"Be true to yourself," Captain reminds me before he and Master Anderson leave the room.

I'm still kneeling when Master Anderson re-enters. "Stand and serve your Master."

I stand and glance up at him briefly.

Master Anderson's dark hair contrasts well with his green eyes. He has a classic, model-like face and a deep, sexy voice that makes you weak inside.

"Undress for me," he orders.

Unlike Baron, Master Anderson doesn't waster time transitioning me into this new dynamic. I gaze at him as I was instructed to do at the Training Center while I take my clothes off. Every movement is meant to entice as I slowly and sensually reveal my body to him.

"Good girl," he growls when I am done. "Which would you like to start with, the toilets or the dishes?"

I stare at him in shock. Seeing a slight smirk move across his lips, I break out in giggles.

"Had ya, didn't I?"

"You did! You had me wondering if one of your kinks was having naked subs do your housecleaning."

He swipes his hair back, laughing. "I could definitely get used to that."

Master Anderson directs me into a formal dining room and tells me to sit. I can smell the delicious odor of baking bread coming from his kitchen.

"I like something light before an intense session," he states before heading into the kitchen.

I sit there alone, the nerves creeping in, wondering what he means by an "intense session".

Master Anderson returns with bowls of tomato bisque and a basket of fresh rolls. He pours us each a tall glass of water, adding, "It's important to keep hydrated."

Sitting down next to me, he smiles. "Dig in."

I can't resist the rolls and grab one, pulling off a piece and eating it. I close my eyes, enjoying the yeasty taste of his warm rolls. "These are incredible."

"My mother's recipe."

"She must be quite a cook."

"My mama did an exceptional job keeping all of us well fed and happy growing up."

"My dad's the cook in our family, but my mom specializes in desserts."

"How about you?"

"I like cooking well enough, but I've never made a soup as good as this."

"It's easy. Just takes the right ingredients."

We both eat in comfortable silence for several minutes, but curiosity leads me to ask, "So about the rules at the Center…"

He chuckles, taking a sip of his soup before answering. "If you are talking about that rule pertaining to trainers not collaring students or alumni, that is set in stone and cannot be changed."

"Then why did you agree to this?"

"Should you and I prove highly compatible, I have no problem leaving the Center just as Thane Davis did. However, my plan would be to start up my own Training Center in Denver. As the boss, I'd get to make the rules," Master Anderson says with a charming grin.

I return his smile. "Captain did mention you were a good businessman."

"I do like a worthy challenge. Captain told me you're planning to take marketing classes this summer."

"I am, and I can't wait to get back to it."

"See? We'd make a good team. I'll run the business and you market the hell out of it for me."

I giggle, taking another sip of that delicious bisque. I now have a better idea why Captain thought we'd be a good match. It's not just a Dom he's looking for, but a man with a stable future.

Master Anderson sets down his spoon and folds his arms. "So, after we're done here, I thought we'd start out with a quick session of my bullwhip." His eyes flash with excitement when he adds, "I want you to feel her *bite*. Then, we'll follow up with a little fire play and see where it leads from there."

My spoon stops midway to my mouth.

"If you're agreeable," he adds.

"I…" I'm already contemplating using my safeword.

"You do realize I'm kidding."

I let out the breath I'm holding and start to laugh. "I had no idea how funny you were. You always seemed so serious at the Training Center."

"If you only knew the shenanigans that go on behind the scenes with the other trainers…" he chuckles.

I take another bite of my roll, seeing Master Anderson in a whole different light.

"The truth is, as much as I would enjoy introducing you to my bullwhip, I know you prefer sensation play. Therefore, we'll start from there and see how far you want to go tonight."

"Thank you…Master."

He winks at me. Over the course of the meal, we end up discussing world events. I'm impressed by his vast body of knowledge, but what I find even more impressive is the fact that he's not arrogant about it. He makes our conversation both easy and entertaining even though my contribution is limited.

"So, it turns out there *is* a serious side to you," I comment after the meal.

"Oh, yes. I'm a complicated beast," he replies, picking up the dishes. "And you are about to meet another side of me altogether, darlin'."

I feel the butterflies start up again.

When Master Anderson returns, I definitely notice a difference. Gone is the easygoing cowboy and, in his place, is the powerful Dominant I've come to know at the Center.

The submissive in me instantly responds when he commands, "Follow me."

I walk behind him, feeling the excitement build as he leads me down a narrow hallway to the back of the house. He unlocks a door at the end, but before he'll let me enter, he says, "Because of your past experience with Liege, I want to emphasize the importance of your safewords tonight. What are they again?"

"Green if I'm feeling good, yellow for slow down, and red if I need you to stop."

"Excellent." He ushers me inside and I am greeted by a room lit with candles. The glow gives it a decidedly romantic feel, contrasting well with the wall covered in BDSM tools on the right. My eyes are immediately drawn to Master Anderson's bullwhip hanging in the very center of the wall, and I shiver.

"There will be no intercourse tonight," he informs me. "I want to determine if you are compatible as my submissive first."

Although I've scened with Master Anderson as my

trainer during practicums, I've never gotten up close and personal with his large "asset". With our obvious difference in physique, I have often wondered how much my body could take of that impressive cock, so having that off the table tonight—so to speak—allows me to concentrate solely on the power exchange.

"Lie on the table, slave," he commands.

It's so different being here in Master Anderson's private playroom as his submissive rather than his student at the Center, and I'm surprised to find myself suddenly feeling shy around him.

"Yes, Master," I answer, walking to the table in the middle of the room. Master Anderson's brand of dominance is definitely more forceful that either Captain's or Baron's, and I tremble a little as I climb up onto the table to lie down on it.

"Let me look at you, slave. Hands at your sides, legs spread."

Master Anderson runs his hand over my naked skin with an admiring gaze, as he explores my body with his light caresses. He then spends a few moments playing with my breasts, rolling my hard nipples between his fingers.

He walks over to the wall and lifts a pink chain with a nipple clamp on each end from a hook. He walks back to me and places it on the table next to my shoulders—but says nothing.

Master Anderson caresses my body again, but this time he concentrates his attention on my pussy. To my frustration, he leaves again, heading to a chest of drawer. Pulling out a razor and shaving cream, he returns to me with a smile as he places them on the table near my pelvis.

I now understand he's letting me know his intentions while he spontaneously decides what the night's festivities will involve.

His hands return to my skin, and I close my eyes as he trails his fingers down my throat. His light touch is causing delightful goosebumps.

I open my eye when I feel him leaning forward, just before our lips connect.

Kissing my former trainer adds a wicked element to this power exchange and I moan softly when his tongue enters my mouth.

Looking into his green eyes, I'm drawn in by the sheer power of his dominance and whisper, "Master…"

He growls under his breath, kissing me with greater passion before leaving me again. This time he chooses a short leather strap from the wall and places it on the table next to my head. I have no idea what he plans to do with the strap, but the placement of it leaves me curious and trembling in anticipation.

Master Anderson positions himself in my line of sight and slowly pulls his black t-shirt over his head. The cut muscles of his chest and abs are a thing to behold, and I grin in appreciation. He raises an eyebrow as he slowly unbuttons his jeans, exposing the fact that he is not wearing any underwear.

I cannot help but stare at his massive cock. It is an impressive sight, and I instinctively lick my lips.

Knowing he has my full attention, Master Anderson moves up to the head of the table. "First, the restraint."

He takes the leather strap and places it across my neck, securing it in place with fasteners in the table. "Enough pressure to make you feel helpless," he states.

My heart skips a beat. It's tight enough that I cannot move my head from side to side and am left staring up at the ceiling—vulnerable and helpless, just like he said. It's an aspect of bondage that I like.

"Color?" he asks.

"Green."

He then picks up the nipple clamps and shows them to me. "Do you trust me?"

I like sensation play, but nipple clamps are uncomfortable and something I have avoided up until now. I gaze at them nervously, and then look up at Master Anderson. This is a test. Do I trust him enough to challenge me? His care and kindness toward me at the Training Center makes me confident in my answer. "Yes, Master."

But my heart begins to race as he plays with one nipple, readying it for the clamp by playing with it until it is hard between his fingers. I hold my breath as he places the cold metal on my nipple and beings tightening it. I whimper when the pressure gets to be too much, and he immediately stops.

Pulling away, he looks down at me with a seductive smile. "Give it time, slave…"

I look up into his eyes with trust and feel the ache slowly beginning to dissipate.

"Color?"

"Green-yellow."

He raises an eyebrow. "Are you ready for the other?"

There is a tinge of fear in answering yes, knowing what it will feel like, but my curiosity spurs me on to comply. "Yes, Master."

Master Anderson readies my other nipple, placing the second clamp onto it. I cringe as he tightens it to the same level of pressure as the other. But I feel an extra connection to him as I stare into those green eyes, waiting for the ache to lessen.

"And now for the fun," he states, rubbing each nipple being squeezed by the device.

He picks up the chain that connects the two nipple clamps and begins playing with it. I squirm in my restraints, my nipples responding to his expert manipulation as he pulls on the chain slightly, mimicking the feel and pressure of two men sucking on my breasts at the same time.

I look up at him in awe, not realizing they could feel so sexy. He grins in satisfaction while he lightly strokes my pussy with his other hand, setting my entire body on fire.

"You're wet, slave."

There's no denying it. "Yes, Master. Thank you."

It's easy to see he enjoys my pleasure. After several minutes, he sets the chain back down on my chest and moves to the end of the table, standing there between my open legs.

"And now for your shave."

I have had a waxing before, but never a shave. There is a dangerous element to it because he is using a razor in such a sensitive area.

It requires an even greater level of trust on my

part…

Before he begins, Master Anderson places his hand on my mound, saying in a husky voice, "I love shaving a woman."

He leaves the room for a moment without explanation. The anticipation builds as I wait for his return, and I smile to myself. It seems that in everything he does, Master Anderson is drawing on and pulling out my submissive side. There is a definite reason he is a trainer at the school.

When Master Anderson returns, he settles down between my legs, spreading them out wide as he wets my skin with a damp cloth before lathering up the area.

Before he begins, he asks, "Do you consent to a shave?"

"Yes, Master."

I hold my breath the first time the razor touches my skin and he scrapes across it. Because of my restraint, I'm left staring up at the ceiling during the shave, unable to see what he is doing gives me a feeling of objectification as I lie here.

Master Anderson is slow and meticulous as he shaves off all my pubic hair. But, oh my God, it tickles when he shaves the sensitive area near my clit, and I have to concentrate hard to keep from squirming. I can tell he enjoys my internal struggle because he chuckles softly every time he makes a pass over the ticklish parts.

Once I am completely bare, he cleans me off.

"I enjoy petting bare pussy, slave. But do you know what I love even more?"

"No, Master."

As I stare up at the ceiling, my eyes wide, as I the feel the sensual caress of his hand on my smooth mound. It sends tingles throughout my entire body, and then…I feel his tongue.

I shudder in pleasure as he teases my clit with his mouth, sucking, licking, and flicking it with that expert tongue. When he sneaks his hand up and begins playing with the chain of the nipple clamps, stimulating my nipples again, I cry out in sheer ecstasy.

"More, more, more!" I beg breathlessly.

"Oh, slave, this is only the beginning…"

Casualties

Captain

After leaving Candy in the capable hands of Anderson, I feel convinced this is a viable match. The man's humor and wit will pair up nicely with Candy's own, and their similar interests in business should bode well for the future.

My mission isn't to find someone for Candy just for now—hell, I could be that for her. No, I want someone she can partner with for a lifetime. Someone I know is worthy of her love and submission.

Ever since the visit to the pet shop, I haven't been able to get Trouper out of my mind. The idea of getting a dog interests me, but rather than purchasing a pup from a store, I head to the nearest animal shelter to save a life.

Unfortunately, I'm informed by the volunteer at the front desk that they have no Australian Shepherds at the kennel so I'm directed to one across town that does.

I sit in LA traffic to get to it, but when I go to the

front desk, the woman tells me, "No, I'm sorry. We don't have any Australian Shepherds."

I sigh in frustration, having made the long trip. "Can you check?"

She gets up and opens the door to the back. I hear several barking dogs as she yells over the din, "Hey Chuck, we got any Australians I don't know about?"

I hear from back in the kennels, "We have one, but she's fifteen years old and was diagnosed with Addison's disease."

The woman looks at me and shrugs. "I'm sorry, the poor dog isn't really adoption material. Would you like me to check the other shelters for one?"

"Can I see her?"

"She isn't expected to live more than a year."

"Can I see her?"

"Of course." She opens the door and yells at Chuck. "Come up here. He'd like to see her."

Chucks walks up from the back to escort me to the dog's kennel. I pass by countless dogs, many looking up at me and wagging their tails hopefully, but when I come to the Australian, I find her curled up in the corner looking completely desolate.

Chuck unlocks the door and her ears twitch, but she doesn't bother to lift her head.

He explains, "She's been this way ever since she arrived. It's like she's given up."

"Why was she surrendered to the pound?"

"If I remember right, the owner passed away."

I look at the dog, which seems lost in grief. "Can you give me some time alone with her?"

"Sure thing. I'll dig up the paperwork on her, if you like."

"Do."

After he leaves, I slowly walk up to the dog. "I know you miss your master, girl..."

I sit down beside her with my back against the cement wall. As I look at the dog with those sad blue and brown eyes, I am overcome with a profound sense of remorse myself.

Memories of the events that led to the deaths of my entire battery invade my mind and I am transported back to that day on the battlefield.

"One of our nation's own DEA agents has been tortured and killed by a well-known drug trafficker in Central America. This is a direct and blatant attack on our country, and it represents a clear and present danger to the security of the United States of America; therefore, I direct that this threat must be dealt with swiftly. This is an act of war."

My battery is part of a covert bilateral mission to take him out and eliminate his entire cocaine operation. When we are done here, there will be nothing left of Javier Garcia but a memory. With intelligence gained by local informants and allied forces already on the ground in that region, we know the location of Javier's facility and the exact day and time he will be arriving to check on production. We have planned a multipronged attack coordinated with artillery support from the host nation.

The day of the mission, a light mist hangs in the air over the triple canopy jungle. It gives the terrain an almost mystical quality as we make our way to the first objective. Many of the veteran troops remark on the similarity with operations they've conducted in Vietnam.

The sound of birds in the canopy of trees above helps to mask the sound of our approach. We have four companies making up the battalion and enter the field with 527 souls onboard with one mission in mind.

Based on our intel, Javier will be visiting his production facility at 1500 hours. I position my battery just behind the ridge, and settle in to wait. I'm confident in our superior firepower and the skill of my men, but the Colonel has additional support ready to assist if needed.

It is imperative that the United States gives a clear and decisive answer to Javier's actions against our government and people.

While we patiently lay in wait, in the hours before Javier is scheduled to arrive, Grapes gives me a nudge in the ribs. "Where do you think we're headed after this?"

"Hopefully, we'll make such an exemplary job of it, we'll all get assigned some R&R in Hawaii."

"Oh yeah, I could see myself spending time with the island girls."

"I bet you can…"

Recently, Grapes has been steering all conversations toward sex, no matter the situation or topic. It's almost become a talent for him.

"So, you're telling me you wouldn't sample the local dishes?" he scoffs.

"Of course, I would. But when I eat, it'll be one dish all night long."

He hits my shoulder. "You really need to start living a little. Think big. Imagine two girls with those big brown eyes and sultry lips kissing your dick as you play with their pussies at the same time, one in each hand..."

His daydreaming is interrupted when I get word that the target has been confirmed and is en route to the site. We have scored big today. Several of his top men are with him.

The plan is for HQ company to crest the ridge while Alpha company moves into position directly west. After a ten-minute artillery barrage to weaken the objective, the main attack on the cartel's compound is set to commence.

I feel the adrenaline pumping as I signal my men to ready their weapons, then I give a confident nod to Grapes.

The attention of every single man on the field is now focused solely on the objective.

I hear reports of movement on our right over the radio, and the hairs on the back of my neck rise. Turning just in time to see the flashes of gunfire begin, I push Grapes to the ground, realizing our trusted military informant is playing both sides and has led us right into an ambush of an army of rebels.

My men return fire while Grapes and I rush to reposition the weapons platoon to strike the new threat. Leaves fall around us as bullets cut through the thick jungle vegetation.

When I hear the distinct *thud* of a RPG-7 slicing

through the jungle foliage, my mouth goes dry. I look at Grapes and our eyes connect just before he is cut in half. The initial explosion strikes a tree directly behind him. His flak jacket is the only thing that shields me from the direct blast as Grape's body splits in two along the bottom edge of his vest. His intestines hit me, along with bits of fractured bone and gristle, as I'm struck by the blast wave and sent flying backwards.

I'm slow to get back on my feet, reeling from the shock. I stare at what's left of my friend, but there is no time to grieve for him. My only goal now is to protect as many of my men as possible by fighting through this ambush.

Understanding the distance and trajectory of the weapon, I order them to attack directly to the west, wanting to engage the enemy and drive them back. We're going to force the rebels to abandon use of their ranged RPG fire on our positions.

I then call in, ordering the additional artillery support fifty meters out from our flank until we close with them.

I fight to remain focused as we fire on the enemy, but the image of Grapes dying in front of my eyes won't stop playing in my mind. I can't wrap my head around the fact he's gone...

When I hear the familiar sound of grenade launchers, I mistakenly believe our reinforcements have arrived. Then I see three of my men blown to pieces by several incoming rounds only fifteen yards from me. Somehow, the enemy has already flanked our position and they have been attacking our company line from the south.

The horrifying reality that we have been pinned

down while a second band of rebels flanks us, begins to set in. As a special "communiqué" to our government, the rebels are killing us with U.S. weapons that they've seized.

The sound of grenades launching from M203s fill the air. Picking up the nearest wounded man, I start dragging him toward safety amid a volley of ammunition, screaming at the top of my lungs for my men to defend south.

Our reinforcements aren't going to make it in time. This is going to be a bloodbath conducted by a much larger force.

My blood runs cold when I hear the familiar *thud* of a grenade launcher firing close by. There is no time to react as it explodes against the tree beside me. I feel the impact and a rapid burst of heat as shrapnel hits my body and thick smoke invades my lungs.

I lose my grip on the man I'm carrying as I fall backwards into darkness. The ringing in my ears blocks out all other sound as I crash into the soil—but I don't even feel myself hitting the ground.

I lay there, stunned, as I watch my men being cut down—their mouths open in soundless screams as they die all around me.

I am powerless as stop the carnage, unable to move, as my body begins to shut down and everything goes black…

I return to the present, overcome with inconsolable grief.

Despite the years, I have never reconciled Grapes' death or the slaughter of my men. That day remains an open wound that claws at my soul.

I sit there on the cement floor, unable to contain the sobs that erupt from deep in my chest. I cover my face with my hands as I start to cry.

I feel a cold nose force its way between my hands as the dog whines softly.

I open my eye and look at her, tears running down my face. The dog whines again, licking my tears. I grab a hold of her and bury my face in her fur.

I force the visions of their deaths from my mind, wanting to regain my composure before Chuck returns—but I'm too late.

"Sir…" he says in a tentative voice, just outside the kennel. "I found the paperwork. Her previous owner named her Echo."

I wipe away the remaining tears and pat Echo on the head before getting up and leaving the kennel to go over her paperwork. Two things strike me as I read through it. First, the autoimmune disease she has is incurable but can be controlled with monthly shots. Second, there is a scribbled note on the margin of the animal's personality file.

If you are reading this, please have mercy and adopt Echo. We recently lost our son and can't afford the medical costs to keep his beloved dog.

The note hits me hard in the chest, and I'm overcome with a sense of sorrow as I look back at the animal.

She was probably his loyal companion for years, and now he's gone and she's been sentenced to death.

"I'm taking her home."

"You understand there will be medical expenses involved if you adopt her."

I look Chuck in the eye. "This dog deserves to die in comfort, not live out her last days in this cement cage before she's euthanized."

"I couldn't agree more. And your name?" Chuck asks, holding out his hand to me.

"Walker."

He thanks me as he shakes my hand, then turns to Echo. "I would have been the one to do it, and I really hated to."

I follow Chuck up to the front to fill out the paperwork and pay the adoption fees. Once it's official, I head back to her kennel and swing the door wide open.

Echo has already retreated to the corner again, her tail tucked between her legs. I walk up to her and lift her into my arms. "You're coming with me, girl."

She starts licking my face once I walk outside and into the fresh air.

I understand that I have agreed to adopt an elderly dog—that I will care for her, only to watch her die. It's a sacrifice I am willing to make so Echo can die with dignity.

I pull up to Anderson's house and pet Echo on the head. "Candy is going to be shocked as hell when she sees you." I give her another pat before I leave. "You stay here."

I suddenly have a twinge of uneasiness as I walk up

to the house. By Anderson's easygoing manner and smile when he answers the door, I have to assume things have gone exceedingly well.

I walk inside to find Candy kneeling on the floor, still naked. I wonder at the reason, and I feel my stomach momentarily drop.

This may be the moment I lose her.

Am I prepared for that?

Yes.

I watch as Anderson places his hand on Candy's head, saying in a formal voice, "I release you back into the care of your Master."

She bows her head lower. "Thank you, Master Anderson."

I can feel a difference in Candy as I place my hand on her head and command, "Stand and serve me, my pet."

When Candy looks up with those big, luminous eyes, I hope I'm wrong. I order her to dress while I discuss the evening with Master Anderson.

"I gave her a shave. I hope you don't mind."

"As long as she gave consent, I have no issues."

"Naturally, consent was given," Anderson replies, his grin growing wider. "I'm not one to wrangle with unwilling pussy."

Candy giggles softly behind me.

I turn back to her, wanting to hear from her how the evening went, so I cut the conversation short. "I hope you don't mind, but I left something in the car that needs attention."

"Not a problem," he says, walking us both to the

door.

Candy turns to Anderson and bows her head. "Thank you for tonight."

"It was my pleasure, Miss Cox," he replies, giving her a private wink.

I escort Candy out, wanting to know the extent of their connection. "I assume things went well?"

Instead of answering, Candy starts running toward the car. "Oh, Captain, you got a dog!"

I look at the car and see Echo sitting in the driver's seat, looking at me.

Candy makes cooing sounds at the dog, then turns around. "When you said you were thinking about getting a dog, I didn't realize you meant so soon. Where did you get her?"

"A shelter."

"That's wonderful!"

"She's old and not expected to live out the year."

Candy looks at me in concern. "I'm so sorry."

"Don't be. I adopted her knowing that."

I'm surprised when Candy throws her arms around me. "What an incredible thing to do."

I wrap my arms around her, relishing the feel of her body pressed against mine, but curiosity won't let me remain silent for long.

"So, tell me. What happened tonight?"

When I see the look of guilt in Candy's eyes, I mentally prepare myself for her answer.

The Unexpected

Candy

I'm surprised and touched by Captain's decision to adopt an older dog and spontaneously hug him. I have no idea what has spurred his sudden interest in getting a dog, but seeing this old pup wagging its tail in his car makes me want to cry.

There is still so much about Captain I don't know, but I enjoy seeing each new layer of his personality revealed as his defenses are peeled away.

"So, tell me. What happened tonight?" he asks.

I can't hide my guilt from Captain, knowing I have failed.

As Captain gets into the car, he lifts the pup and places her in the back seat. He then looks at me. "Well?"

I can barely look him in the eye when I apologize. "I'm sorry…"

"A connection was made?"

"Yes and no."

He looks at me, confused. "What is the apology

for?"

I glance down at my lap and sigh. "I'm sorry for failing, Captain."

He puts his finger under my chin and forces me to look him in the eye. "What happened?"

I frown, hating to admit it. "As much as I enjoyed experiencing Master Anderson's brand of dominance, there came a point when I hesitated." A tear falls from my eye when I confess, "And that's when I failed."

"How?"

"I didn't use my safeword. Master Anderson had to call it for me."

"Thank God for that," he states with relief.

I feel thoroughly humiliated, knowing it's a mistake I shouldn't have made, given my level of experience, but Captain takes my hand.

"I'm grateful for Anderson's perceptiveness. He ensured my sub was well cared for tonight."

"He was extraordinarily kind to me," I agree, still feeling the sting of humiliation when I remember how he had to stop midway through the scene.

"Would you like to try again, knowing what you know now?"

I shake my head. "He and I talked afterward and came to the conclusion that as much as we enjoy each other's company, we're not compatible as a D/s couple."

I'm relieved when I don't see disappointment in Captain's eyes after telling him that.

Instead, he starts the car and says, "You should feel no shame, my pet. You've gained valuable insight into what you need in a Dominant. It'll make things easier as we move on to the next one."

I look back at the dog. She only seems to have eyes for Captain. It warms my heart. It's as if she understands that he rescued her.

I can relate, I think as I look back at Captain.

I feel the same way myself.

Captain is persistent in his mission to find me a suitable Dom and sets up the next one the following weekend.

This time, however, I know exactly who the Dom is. Tonight, I will be scening with Tono Ren Nosaka, the Kinbaku Master.

I have partnered with him before at The Haven and have had only good experiences with the Japanese Dom. Captain feels certain Tono can not only provide me with the level of dominance I need, but a stable future, as well.

He's right. While Tono has a gentle style, his dominance is still intense.

In honor of the world-renowned Master, Captain orders that I dress in something special. I am delighted when Captain comes to pick me up and smiles when he sees me. "You look especially fetching tonight, my pet."

I run my hands over the pink kimono-style top I've chosen for the occasion. "I thought it spoke Japanese but still reflected me."

"I'm sure Nosaka will appreciate your unique style."

Although I've been looking forward to this evening,

I woke up this morning feeling nervous, and have been anxious the entire day. I let out a sigh as Captain helps me into the car.

He glances at me, looking concerned. "Is something wrong?"

I shake my head, but immediately roll my eyes, knowing I need to be honest with him. "I'm not sure, Captain. I've felt antsy all day, but I'm certain it has nothing to do with Tono because I've been looking forward to scening with him tonight."

"I've seen the joy on your face when you were bound in his rope," he agrees. "It's one of the reasons I chose him for you. However, I'd be happy to call and cancel, if you like."

"Oh, no! I definitely want to go, it's just that I've been full of a nervous energy I can't explain."

Captain nods, a slight smile on his lips. "I'd take that as a good sign, if I were you, pet."

My heart always melts when he calls me his pet. It thrilled me the first time, and still has power over me now.

I play with his temporary collar around my neck. I love the light pressure of it against my throat because it acts as a subtle reminder of his dominance. Captain notices me touching the collar but says nothing, returning his eyes to the road.

I understand these sessions with other Doms are meant to open my eyes to what's possible but, so far, each encounter has only made me more certain that Captain is my one.

Despite his suggestion that my nerves indicate something special is going to happen tonight, I'm confident my evening with Tono will be no different.

When Captain pulls up to his home, I find the simple landscaping beautiful. The front yard has a rock garden, which is accented by uniquely shaped trees and ornamental shrubbery lining the path to the house.

"Very Zen-like," I comment as we walk up to the door.

"It is unusual but attractive," Captain agrees.

I glance at him, wondering what he is thinking and, more importantly, what he is feeling. Although he's bound and determined to find me a Dom, it's obvious Captain feels the same way about me as I do him.

Surely, this must be difficult, but his face never betrays any negative emotions. Instead, I catch him smiling at me as if he's enjoying this strange adventure we're on together.

Captain rings the doorbell, and stands with his hands behind his back. I don't know if he realizes how sexy that stance is, and I'm half-tempted to sneak a kiss and purr in his ear.

Tono greets us dressed in a stylish black kimono. He addresses Captain first, as per formal protocol. "It is good to see you again, Captain Walker."

"Likewise, Nosaka. Candy and I appreciate you agreeing to this arrangement."

Tono's attention turns to me, and I find myself blushing unexpectedly as I gaze into his chocolate brown eyes.

"Good evening, Miss Cox."

I bow my head in respect, overwhelmed by the man's

calming presence.

Tono gestures us both inside. As I pass by him, I feel an unexpected rush of adrenaline. I can't explain the reason and choose to distract myself by studying the inside of his home.

I appreciate the open feel to it. There are only a few walls, the focus of the house being the large glass doors that lead to the Japanese garden out back. I find it odd that our surroundings are calm and peaceful, but my sense of anxiousness has actually increased.

It isn't a negative feeling, however—more like a building of anticipation.

Tono gestures for the two of us to sit on the couch. "Can I get either of you something to drink?"

"There is no reason to waste pleasantries on me. This isn't exactly a social call," Captain states with a smile. "I'm only staying long enough to ensure Candy is comfortable."

My heart flutters, knowing he is concerned for me. "I'm good, Captain."

He turns back to Tono. "Since I've had the pleasure of watching you scene with Candy before, I have no reservations about leaving her in your care. What time would you like me to return?'"

Tono stares at me thoughtfully for several moments before answering. "I'm anticipating a four-hour session."

I can't believe I'm about to experience four hours of intense connection with the famous Kinbaku Master.

"I'll return then."

Captain cradles my face in his hands, kissing my forehead tenderly. "Enjoy Nosaka's gift."

He nods to Tono before striding toward the door to let himself out.

The antsy feeling intensifies when I find myself alone with the bondage Master.

Suddenly, I find myself unsure what to say or how to act around him. It's as if all my submissive training has gone out the window, so I just stand there awkwardly.

Rather than stating a command, Tono studies me.

The prolonged silence is unsettling, and I wonder if I have failed to follow some unspoken protocol.

Rather than continuing to stand there looking foolish, I ask, "Would you like me to kneel, Tono?"

"No," he answers in a smooth voice, easing my fears of having disappointed him. "I would like you to sit at the table."

While I walk to the table, Tono heads to his kitchen and puts a teapot on the stove to boil. I settle on the floor next to the low-lying table, charmed by his traditional Japanese furniture.

I watch as he makes tea, telling my nerves to quiet down.

When it's done, he carries the teapot over to the table, along with two cups. Before sitting down, he opens up the sliding glass door to let a gentle breeze of night air flow into the house.

Tono sits across from me and gracefully pours the pale green liquid into one cup, sliding it over to me before pouring another for himself.

He remains silent as he looks at me, bringing the cup to his lips to take a sip.

I follow his example, but blow on the steaming liquid

before taking my first taste. The green tea has a naturally sweet flavor to it, and I smile. "This is very good."

He only nods, his gaze unfaltering and intense.

Normally, Tono is not so mysterious, and I wonder at the change.

It isn't until we've finished the tea that he finally speaks again. "You seem unsettled, Miss Cox."

I'm actually relieved to talk about it. "I am, but I can't for the life of me explain why."

The Japanese Master looks deeply into my eyes as if searching for the answer I am unable to voice. "I will start with a simple binding, then we'll progress from there."

"That sounds wonderful, Tono."

"Good. Tonight, because of this unique arrangement, I will address you as Amai."

I like the way it sounds and ask, "What does it mean?"

"Sweet—like your name."

I blush, touched by the perfect sub name he has given me.

Tono stands up and commands, "Undress completely before you kneel on the mat." He nods toward the jute mat in the center of the room.

I stand up gracefully as I have been taught, but my hands tremble as I take off my clothes. I have been naked in front of him before, but now I feel unexplainably silly and shy.

His eyes never leave me as I undress and take my place on the mat.

Tono walks over to the sound system and turns on

soothing flute music before settling down behind me with a length of jute in his hand. He sets it on the mat, but rather than wrap his arms around me as he has done before, Tono glides his hands just centimeters above my skin, never touching me as he explores my body.

Even without skin-to-skin contact, I swear I can feel the warmth of Tono's gentle caress. He lets out a low groan as one hand hovers over the center of my chest. I involuntarily shiver, my entire being focused on that point.

"Heartbreak," he whispers in my ear.

It's as if that simple word has unlocked a floodgate of emotion inside me. From deep within, a rush of sadness washes over me and I begin sobbing.

Tono's strong arms wrap me in a tight embrace, and he murmurs words of comfort as he begins to rock back and forth.

I cannot stop the loud, desperate cry of mourning that escapes from the depths of my soul.

Tono tightens his hold, helping to carry me through the grief. When I finally stop crying, I collapse against his arms, the tears still flowing unchecked down my cheeks.

"Who is it you mourn for?" he asks.

I close my eyes. Ethan's face is as clear to me as if he were standing beside me. "Someone I loved very much."

"A tragic separation," he states.

I only nod, unable to speak, the lump in my throat too big and painful.

"You are bound to that moment."

"Yes…" I whisper.

"Why?"

I shake my head, the sobs starting up again as I relive that moment when Ethan pushed me out of the way of the oncoming truck. As I was thrown to safety, I had no idea his life was ending.

The pain becomes too great and I struggle against Tono's tight embrace, but he continues to hold me, murmuring for me to be still.

I quiet down as he rocks back and forth, but my emotions are raw and too painful to bear. "Why have you done this to me?" I cry.

He chuckles softly. "This was not what I had planned, but it's what your heart needs."

"I wanted to spend time in your rope, not this," I whimper.

"But your soul will not allow it—this pain needs to be set free."

I shake my head, not liking this unwanted turn of events.

"I feel your resistance, but I ask you to trust me, Amai."

The last thing I want is to face the guilt I feel over Ethan's death. In protest, I struggle again to break away from his grasp.

However, Tono's grip is like iron, and I'm finally forced to stop fighting, too tired to resist.

"This blackness you carry…what is it?"

"Ethan died because of me." The burden of that truth crushes my soul.

"How?" Tono gently prods.

I can barely speak the words out loud, my guilt is so great and heavy. "He died saving me."

I imagine the look of terror that must have been on

Ethan's face as the truck barreled straight into him. I cry out to Ethan, "I'm so sorry I killed you."

I'm inconsolable now, sobbing so violently I can barely breathe, trapped in that moment with no way to change it. Tono continues to rock me, his chin resting against my shoulder. He offers no words, only his protective embrace.

It feels as if the pain has no end, but my body can't handle the continuous onslaught and I eventually fall into an almost subspace-like trance.

In that state, I see the scene play out again. Ethan stares at the truck heading straight for him, but he does not have a look of terror. He's not looking at the truck at all. Ethan is looking at me with a look of relief.

For the briefest moment, I feel his presence as if it is as real as Tono's is now. As he fades, his smile is the last thing I see.

Although my tears still fall, the warmth of his smile stays with me and I feel the truth in my heart. It would have been the same had I been the one to die and he the one to live. It didn't matter who lived, as long as one of us did.

Ethan did not face his death with fear. He faced it with hope.

I take in a deep breath, filling my lungs.

I stare outside at Tono's beautiful garden while I'm filled with peace, finally able to accept the gift Ethan has given me.

I live so we both can live on.

Holding onto the guilt has only tarnished the enormity and sanctity of his gift.

Thank you, Ethan.

I'm completely spent and am weak and exhausted after such an emotional release.

Tono lifts me up and carries me to the bedroom, laying me on his bed. He then lies beside me, wrapping an arm around me and pulling me close.

I feel like I'm floating on a cloud of well-being.

"Tono..."

"Yes, Amai?"

"This was the last thing I wanted, but I'm grateful to you." I turn my head and gaze into his kind eyes. "I'm sorry I didn't serve you tonight."

"You did exactly as I asked."

"You've changed me, Tono."

"I only acted as a catalyst."

"Please...how can I repay you?" I beg in earnest.

He brushes my cheek with his finger. "I am fully satisfied with tonight, and your Master is coming."

"No..." I say in disbelief. "It hasn't been that long,"

The doorbell rings, announcing that I'm wrong, and I look at Tono sheepishly.

"Dress while I speak with your Master," he commands with a smile.

My movements are sluggish as I redress, but my heart it filled with joy as I listen to the two men speaking.

I understand now why Captain says he lives for his men.

That is my duty to Ethan.

I come out of Tono's bedroom and see Captain staring at me with a look of...acceptance.

I'm sure he believes something else has occurred tonight, but he has no idea—and I can't wait to tell him!

The Mission

Captain

After leaving Candy with Nosaka, I'm struck by the same feeling she expressed having earlier. There is something different about tonight's pairing. Her excitement leads me to believe he is the one—and I am fine with that.

Nosaka is not only a good man, but his gentle personality is exactly what I know Candy needs. As an experienced Dom, he will challenge her with the demands of his jute bondage, and I know she will grow under his care.

Rather than a desperate feeling of loss, I have a sense of fate. It's as if this was meant to be.

I look at Echo, who is sitting in my seat. "Over," I command.

She instantly jumps into Candy's seat, looking at me expectantly.

It seems fate has orchestrated all of this all and I am grateful.

I drive to Gallant's, wanting to share my thoughts with him. He doubted my wisdom, and I will enjoy proving him wrong.

I put Echo on a leash, planning to leave her outside, as I have never seen an animal in Gallant's house. Ena answers the door and immediately bows her head to me before smiling at the dog.

"I was told you saved a life."

I look down at Echo and smirk. "It's mutual."

"I'm sorry to tell you this, Captain Walker, but my husband is seriously allergic to dog hair. I can't let her inside."

"Not an issue." I hold up the leash in my hand. "Echo's perfectly content to sit under a tree."

The two girls pop around the corner and squeal in unison. "A dog!"

I immediately hold out my hand, telling them to stop. "You need to approach Echo slowly. She doesn't know you yet."

I noticed Echo's tail in down as I introduce her to each child. Within a few seconds, however, her tail is up and wagging as she licks the youngest.

"Is it okay if they play with her in the backyard?" Ena asks.

I look down at the two giggling girls getting a tongue bath. "I think Echo would prefer it."

After setting her free in the backyard, I enter the house and wash my hands at the kitchen sink.

Gallant walks up behind me. "A dog?"

"A companion."

He looks at me with interest. "Is there any particular

reason you need a companion?"

"There appears to be," I answer smugly. "As you know, I took your advice, and it turns out I was right."

"Ah…who is the chosen Dom, then?"

"Nothing official yet, but I have a strong feeling that Nosaka will win the day."

"How does Candy feel about that?"

"There was something different about her when I dropped her off. I had the same feeling as well, which leads me to believe that after tonight, she'll have a Master who will be able to support her through the years."

Gallant looks at me questioningly. "How do you feel?"

"I feel fine, like this was meant to be. That's why I'm so certain."

"And you will be able to let her go?"

"Absolutely. Hell, that's what I've been working toward this entire time."

He presses his lips together before saying, "I've got to hand it to you, Captain. If she chooses Ren Nosaka, not only will you be proven right, but you'll also prove that Candy was wrong."

I frown. "No, she wasn't wrong to love me. She simply could do better."

Gallant nods, saying nothing.

"Why do I get the impression you're holding something back?"

"Not at all. I'm just surprised." Gallant looks out at the girls petting Echo. "So, you'll replace Candy with the dog?"

"Of course not," I huff. "I'll move on, but I hope to

stay in contact with Candy and Nosaka, so I can see their children grow up."

Gallant gives me an odd look.

"What? Do you think it's strange I hope to remain a small part of her life?"

"No..."

"Spit it out, Gallant."

He shakes his head. "I can't."

"What? Why are you holding back on me?"

"I can't say. It's a privacy issue."

"I cannot begin to guess what you're hinting at, but I assume it has to do with Candy."

"I suggest you talk to her. Be open about what your thoughts are concerning the future."

"Is something wrong?"

"Not wrong, but I can't say anything about it."

I'm very unsatisfied with our conversation, but Gallant is right to protect Candy's privacy. I can't fault him for that, no matter how much it frustrates me.

Changing the topic, I tell him in a smug voice, "You will be owing me after this."

He smiles. "Yes, I know. Something tells me you won't go easy on me."

I shake my head with a slow smile.

The backdoor slides open and Gallant's oldest cries out, "Daddy, can we get a dog?"

I can't help but laugh.

Ena enters the kitchen and corrects her daughter before Gallant can answer. "You know your father is allergic. It's unkind to ask."

The youngest enters, adding her two cents. "But,

Daddy, dogs are so cute!"

Ena shoos them both outside and has a private discussion with the girls that neither of us can hear.

"I guess it's time to invest in some pet goldfish," I joke.

He sighs, looking at his daughters' sad faces as Ena continues to talk to them. "We already have fish…"

"I hear snakes make great pets."

He gives me an unamused smile.

We retire to his study to talk until my appointed time to fetch Candy.

"Are you still feeling at peace?" Gallant asks.

"Even more so."

He slaps me on the back. "Then I hope the best for you both."

As I lift Echo into the car, Gallant calls out, "Make sure to speak with Candy."

I raise my hand to let him know I've heard, but I suspect it won't be necessary after tonight.

I ring the doorbell, but it takes a few minutes for Nosaka to answer it. He invites me in and tells me that Candy is readying herself.

When I ask how the evening went, he answers, "I think it's best if she tells you herself."

I wonder what that means until she emerges from Tono's bedroom with a look of joy on her face.

So, I was right…

Tono looks to Candy with tenderness. "We had an unexpected evening, one I'm honored to have shared with your submissive."

I look at Candy, and she is positively beaming. I'm grateful she isn't trying to hide how she feels about Nosaka. It would have disappointed me if she had.

As we make our way to the car, Candy grabs my hand excitedly. "Oh, Captain, this was the most incredible night of my life! Everything has changed. Tono changed me."

"I'm glad to hear it," I answer, genuinely pleased to see her so happy.

"At first, I was so mad at Tono for forcing me, but then..." she trails off, looking back at the door.

The hairs rise on the back of my neck and I spit out, "He forced you?" I start walking back to the door, ready to teach Nosaka to respect my woman.

Candy pulls my arm, laughing. "No, no! It was wonderful. He was wonderful."

Now, I suddenly hate the man. "Explain yourself, and quickly."

Candy wraps her small arms around me in a hug. "I love how protective you are."

I pull away from her. "Answer me, Candy."

"We didn't scene tonight. Not even one knot."

I suddenly have visions of them spending hours having vanilla sex and, for some reason, that infuriates me. "Clarify what you mean."

Candy grins. "I have been waiting to see that look on your face this entire time."

I frown, barking, "What face?"

"This is the first time I've seen you look jealous, and it melts my heart."

I know Candy is not a cruel person but, right now, she is being anything but kind so I glare at her.

Candy laughs gently. "Captain, I spent the last four hours crying. Tono helped me face my guilt over Ethan."

Now she has my attention. "What did he do?"

"I'm not sure, really. But all the angst I was feeling today bubbled up and erupted before we even began. What was supposed to be an evening of bondage became my night of freedom."

Her eyes sparkle with an inner light I have never seen before.

"I'm happy for you, pet. However, I don't understand."

She bursts into a huge grin. "All the guilt I've carried since Ethan's death…it was pointless. Ethan…" Tears come to her eyes. "He died to save us—him and me." She wraps her arm around me again. "All this time, I didn't understand what you meant when you said you were living for your men, but I get it now. Your life means that they live on."

I can tell by the way she's talking she is light-years ahead of me. I'm mired in the guilt of their deaths, and I still can't see a way through it. However…I'm grateful Nosaka was able to give her that gift.

Truly, he is worthy of being her Dom.

"And your feelings toward Nosaka now?"

"I will forever be grateful to him."

"But do you love him?" I ask, needing to hear her say it.

Her smile widens. "No. I love *you*."

I stare at her in surprise, not expecting that answer.

"Captain, tonight I have had a point of clarity so powerful and real that I feel different, but the one thing that has not changed is my love for you. Tonight, it's even stronger."

This is not what's supposed to happen...

"It doesn't have to end here. I will look for another Dom," I assure her.

She takes my hands. "No matter who you choose, they will never be you, and you are the only person I want to submit to."

I take a deep breath. Gallant advised me to speak with her, convinced there was something I needed to know.

"Let me be frank. I'm old, and while I technically could have a child at my age, I have zero interest in raising one."

I see a flash of pain flit across her eyes and regret that I am the cause. As much as I hate to do it, Gallant is right. This is the conversation we needed to have.

"Captain, there's something I never told you because I didn't think it mattered to you."

The look on her face has me worried, and I instinctively cradle her cheek with my hand, wanting to comfort her. "What is it?"

"I can't have children. I was born with a defect that makes me barren."

The idea that little miniatures of Candy won't be running around her feet saddens me. "I'm so sorry, my pet."

She clasps my hand pressed against her face, and smiles up at me. "I've known since I was a teenager, but you're the first man I've met who I knew wouldn't care. Don't you see how perfect we are for each other?"

I do, but I'm hesitant to claim her. I look into Candy's eyes, my head wanting to convince her otherwise, but my heart won't let me.

"This is what you want?"

"Yes, more than anything else in the world."

I lay out my uniform and stare at it. Not that long ago, I had no reason to don it once more. As I dress, I think about the exceptional woman whose devotion brought me to this point. I am the luckiest man on earth.

Today is the day I collar my submissive.

I put on the eye patch Candy gave me before slipping on my jacket. Turning toward the mirror, I look at the reflection. This is who I am now—a man of fifty-six years who carries the scars of the past on his body and in his soul—but who now faces a new and satisfying future with Candy.

Falling in love—what an odd emotion to experience at my age. I pick up the box containing the collar I had made for her and smile to myself.

Last night, Candy experienced life-changing healing under the care of Ren Nosaka. She seemed more joyous and confident than I'd ever seen her. When she said I was the only man she would submit to, I believed her.

My mission to find her another Dom has turned out to be not just a journey for Candy, but also for me. I'm convinced now that Gallant knew this would be the outcome, but made his proposal knowing I needed to come to my own conclusions.

Clever man...

I drive to Candy's apartment, not with a sense of anxiousness as I did the first time, but with confidence. I knock on her door and stand back, waiting for her to answer.

She's not expecting me.

The conversation we had last night was left open-ended. Today, I will give her my answer.

I hear Candy run to the door. She freezes when she opens it, her eyes growing wide. "Oh, Captain..."

"May I come in?"

"Please," she answers, inviting me in before closing the door. She stares at my uniform before looking up at me. "Does this mean...?"

I take the thin box and open it, revealing the delicate pink collar with a gold lock. "I had this made especially for you."

She lets out a small gasp as she stares at it and asks, "May I touch it?"

In answer, I lift it from the box and hand it to her. "Please do."

Candy's hands tremble slightly as she looks at her new collar.

"It is studded with diamonds, and I had the lock engraved with something you once told me."

She looks at the gold lock, smiling as she reads the

word on the front engraved in an elegant script. "Love."

"Look on the back," I tell her.

She turns it over. "Has no limits." She nods, tears filling her eyes.

"Candy, it is my intention to collar you as my exclusive submissive. Do you accept?"

Without hesitation, she kneels before me with her head bowed, holding up the collar with both hands.

Kneeling beside her, I take off the temporary collar and lay it on the floor. Taking the new one from her hands, I solemnly place it around Candy's neck, clicking the lock into place.

"You are my cherished pet. As your Master, I vow to protect, love, and guide you. This collar is a symbol of my ownership and our commitment to one another."

Candy gazes up at me with adoration. "Captain, I gratefully accept this symbol of your ownership and I will wear it proudly."

I stand up and help her to her feet.

Holding the key to her lock, I continue. "I will wear this key as a symbol of our commitment to you. I promise to respect and honor you in my dominance over you. Your happiness is my prime objective."

I take a chain from my pocket and slide the key onto it, commanding, "Place it around my neck."

Candy takes it from me, her hands trembling slightly as she lifts it over my head and the key settles against my chest, close to my heart. A tear escapes her eye as she touches it. "And promise to honor and love you as I serve you, Captain. My submission to you is freely given and I will respect your dominance over me as we become one."

I lift her chin and kiss her deeply. "I claim you as mine, Candy Cox."

She smiles, having never looked as beautiful as she does right now. "I am happy to be yours forever and always, Charles Walker."

I lift Candy up and carry her to the bedroom, wanting to make the same vow to her body.

Setting her down on the bed, I pull the gold leash out of my pocket and place it on the nightstand. I then command her to undress me.

She bites her lip in anticipation as she moves to the end of the bed. "May I admire you for a moment, Captain?"

I indulge her, noting the look of lustful approval in her eyes. This woman has the ability to make me feel not only desirable, but also fully a man.

My cock aches as she reaches up to undo the first button on my jacket.

"Wait," I tell her, suddenly wanting to watch this beautiful creature do it with nothing on but my collar.

I lift off her shirt, pleased to find she is not wearing a bra. Unzipping her short skirt, I slide it down, along with her panties. After I have her completely naked, I pick up the leash. Her eyes widen as I click it to her new collar.

Wrapping the leash several times in my hand to tighten my hold, I lean down and kiss her. "Now you may undress me, pet."

Candy kneels on the bed, looking at me with those round, luminous eyes as she begins unbuttoning my jacket.

I look down the line of her back to her sexy ass, enjoying the view as she undoes each button. Spreading the jacket open, and I switch the leash from one each hand to the other as she slips the fabric off my shoulders, before solemnly handing it to me.

I reach over and lay it on the nightstand, turning back to her.

Candy starts on the tie next, untying it with a look of delight as she pulls it through my shirt collar. She puts it in her mouth and offers it to me playfully. I kiss her on the forehead before taking it from her.

My shirt is next, followed quickly by my undershirt. Candy sits back on her haunches to look at me and says with admiration, "My handsome Master."

I feel a deep sense of satisfaction hearing her call me Master, knowing she is mine and mine alone.

I watch as she slowly unbuckles my belt, sliding it through the belt loops. She hands it to me with a shy look. There are a lot of things a man can do with a belt, but tonight it will remain on the nightstand.

My desire is to dominate her sweet body with love and attention.

She unbuttons my trousers next, then slowly unzips them. I groan as she eases my shaft from my briefs and looks up at me. "May I?"

"You may."

I close my eye when her warm lips encase my cock and she begins sucking.

Sweet heaven...

It doesn't take long before my shaft demands the warmth of her pussy. I pull on her leash and command her to turn around so that her sexy ass faces me.

She lowers her torso onto the bed and looks back at me, mewing softly.

I shake my head, thoroughly taken by her flirtatious charm.

I growl seductively, as I press my body into hers. "Now, it's time to claim what is mine…"

As One

Candy

Laying in Captain's arms as his one-and-only submissive fills my heart with overwhelming joy.

I sigh in contentment and turn my head toward him, stating, "I'm yours, Captain."

He tightens his grip around me. "All mine, pet."

"You have made me so happy today."

With a smile on his lips, Captain grazes his fingers along my cheekbone. "I am a profoundly lucky man."

I'm truly amazed to find myself here. "It's hard to believe all the twists and turns it took to bring us together."

"I will forever be grateful for the day I ran into Gallant and his wife."

I shake my head, thinking back on that chance meeting. "I never imagined the interesting path our chance meeting would lead me down."

I nod. "Even though Ethan's death eventually led me to Liege, it also allowed Brie to find me. She changed the course of my life when she invited me to attend the Submissive Training Center. It was there that I found you."

"No, it was *your* unwavering belief and persistence that brought us to this point."

I trail my fingers over the collar around my neck. "I'm actually grateful you insisted on the temporary collar first. I've gained so much from each of the Doms you selected for me."

"I began that search solely to spare you from heart-ache."

"And I love you for that," I tell him, kissing him tenderly.

"I have one more question for you tonight."

"Anything."

"Would you move in with me to make this a 24/7 partnership?"

My heart flutters at the thought. "Yes! That's been my heart's desire since our first scene together."

"How do you think your parents will react to you moving into my home?"

I chuckle. "I'm pretty sure they saw this coming."

"It won't cause a strain between you?" he asks, concerned for me.

The fact that he cares endears him even more to me. "No, Captain. My parents have always said they want me to be happy and just look at me now!" I grin. "This girl couldn't be any happier than I am right now."

He plays with the new collar around my neck. "And, if they ask about this?"

"I'll gauge how much to tell them, but I'm proud to

wear your collar. I would never deny the significance of it, if they ask."

"It may be only leather but, make no mistake, I will love and protect you until my dying breath."

I put my finger to his lips. "That won't happen for a long, long time."

He grabs my wrist to kiss my fingers. "Agreed. This old man has too much to live for now." Captain wraps his arms around me again, nuzzling my neck. "Tomorrow we will revisit the pet shop where we made our formal introductions."

I can't believe how incredibly romantic he is and purr with delight.

Once I officially move in with Captain, I notice sweet Echo treating me as an extension of Captain even though, first and foremost, he remains her Master and main focus.

As a special treat, we take Echo with us to our favorite pet shop to find her some new toys. The dog is unfailingly loyal to Captain, obeying his every command and eager to please her Master—something she and I have in common.

There's a special bond between the two, even when he gives her the shots she needs to stay well. Echo takes them without flinching, wagging her tail afterward as if she understands Captain is helping her.

It is a beautiful thing to witness—this trust she has

for him.

Even though Echo's gray with age, she retains her puppy heart. At the pet shop, she settles on a stuffed squirrel with a squeaker inside. Captain and I look at each other, knowing the sound is going to drive us crazy, but Echo's enthusiasm for the toy leaves us no choice but to buy it.

"Now for you," Captain tells me with a glint in his eye. "What catches my pet's attention?"

Being Captain's submissive, I'm a seriously spoiled girl. I know there is nothing he wouldn't give me. At the same time, there is nothing I wouldn't give him. We are the perfect balance, and he makes me feel completely loved.

I look over the large aisle of cat toys and find a particularly cute one that has a butterfly attached to a wire. The motion of the mechanical toy mimics the real insect as it flies around in a circular pattern. It's so adorable and silly, I know I will have hours of fun batting at it and playing with it as his kitten.

I point to the box and smile shyly.

"Perfect for you," Captain states as he picks one up. He also grabs a set of little pink and purple fuzzy balls for me to chase later—a sexy game of catch-the-mouse.

I love that I can be so carefree around him without an ounce of judgement or shame. I press my cheek again his broad arm and rub against it like a real kitten, purring softly.

"You don't know what that does to me," he murmurs. Looking down at his crotch, he commands, "Down boy."

A more perfect man I will never find…

The Gallants invite us to dinner in celebration of my recent collaring. Captain insists on arriving early so he can speak alone with Mr. Gallant before dinner begins.

While the two men retire to the study, I head off to see if I can assist Ena with dinner. The aromas coming from her kitchen are absolutely mouthwatering.

I'm surprised to find her two daughters already there, the three of them working as a unit, each knowing their task without being asked. I truly admire Ena as a mother.

She is respectful of her children, but still demanding. It's made the girls exceedingly mature for their age, and I know Captain has a definite soft spot for them, although he doesn't normally care for children.

"Ena, is there anything I can help with?" I ask.

She turns and greets me with a warm smile. "We're nearly ready, Miss Cox. However, if you would like to fill the glasses with water, that would be lovely."

"Thank you," I reply, truly grateful to be included.

Once we're all finished with preparations, Ena tells the girls it's time to invite the men to join us at the table. Once the two are out of earshot, she tells me, "We have been looking forward to this dinner for quite some time. Sir Davis and Brie have been extremely busy, and we wanted to give you time alone as a newly-formed D/s couple."

I play with the collar around my neck. "I've been living on cloud nine ever since Captain officially collared me."

"It is a stunning piece of art, and your smile matches it perfectly." She gracefully leans down to give me a hug, which highlights the significant difference in our height. Despite her regal stature, Ena has never once made me feel small.

We hear the girls returning with the men, and she quickly whispers, "My husband and I wish you both all the best."

Once the girls escort Mr. Gallant and Captain into the dining room, Ena tells them, "Thank you for your help, girls. Head upstairs and play until we call you back down."

They give me a playful wave and Captain a formal salute before leaving.

"You have raised gracious children," Captain compliments after they're gone.

Mr. Gallant grasps Ena's hand and smiles. "My wife has instilled everything I love about her into our girls. They couldn't have a better example of what to live up to."

Captain turns to Ena. "Then my compliment must go to you."

Ena shakes her head, gazing lovingly at her husband. "My husband is far too modest. It is *his* leadership that has given our children a foundation they can thrive in."

I find it sweet that they hold such high regard for each other.

The doorbell rings and Mr. Gallant insists on us remaining seated as he goes to answer the door.

I sit, listening to the familiar voices conversing. "Good evening, Mr. Gallant," Sir Davis states in his commanding voice.

"Good evening, Sir Davis, and welcome, Miss Bennett. It's a pleasure to have you join us tonight."

I sit and listen to the conversion, buzzing with excitement as I wait for Brie to enter the room!

Mr. Gallant leads them to the formal dining room and as soon as Brie sees Captain, she bursts into a smile, calling out his name.

Captain seems slightly amused by her reaction, knowing Brie hasn't noticed me yet. "Miss Bennett, it's good to see you again," he answers in a formal tone.

I wait patiently for Brie to notice who is sitting next to him. Her face lights up when our eyes meet.

"Oh, my goodness, Candy! I didn't expect to see you here, too."

Brie turns to Sir Davis. "May I go and hug her, Sir?"

Sir Davis and Brie have developed a much more formal D/s relationship than Captain and I have, prompting Mr. Gallant to inform Brie, "In my home, we do not adhere to strict formalities. Consider tonight a vanilla setting."

Brie looks surprised and glances at Sir Davis, who gives her a slight nod, the two silently agreeing to relax their protocol for the evening.

I hold out my arms to Brie and we hug each other tight. I'm tickled her eyes are riveted on my sparkling new collar.

"Seeing you again is like getting an extra birthday present, Candy. I've wondered what happened to you after you finished training," Brie shares.

I blush, looking over at Captain. "My first auction, I was introduced to Captain, and I have been captivated ever since."

Captain pats the chair beside him, wanting me to sit beside him while he explains to Brie, "If you remember the night you and I shared together, Miss Bennett, then you may recall how I said your blonde classmate was better suited to me."

Brie nods. "I remember the night well, Captain, but not for that reason."

He chuckles. "That is kind of you to say, but I was rather blunt with you. I want you to know you were correct. The outer shell of a woman does not matter. It is the heart that defines her."

He looks at me with such admiration, my heart feels like it's about to burst. "I have never encountered such a loyal or tenderhearted creature." Petting my hair lightly, he adds, "She also happens to be a comely little thing, as well."

I close my eyes, trying to hold back my teary emotions as I lean into his caress.

I am so thoroughly and utterly in love with this man...

"To be honest, Candy," Brie tells me, "when I saw you scening with Tono at The Haven a while back, I thought you two might make the perfect couple. I never suspected that Captain would be the one to capture your heart."

You can tell by the look on her face that she realizes how rude that may sound and immediately adds, "But he's a most wonderful choice!"

I'm not offended in the least and tell her, "Captain wanted me to be certain, and he scheduled sessions with several notable Doms before agreeing to collar me."

"Youth should not be wasted on one as old as I," Captain laughs.

I shake my head as I smile at my Master. "Fortunately, he came to the same conclusion I did." I caress his scarred cheek as we lock gazes. "You see, I was born to be his pet."

Brie suddenly looks distraught. "Did I miss the formal collaring ceremony? I'm sorry. We've been so busy—"

Captain answers for me. "No, Miss Bennett. I have no need for such pomp and circumstance. The commitment we made in private is just as binding as any communal ceremony."

"I quite agree," Sir Davis states.

Brie looks at me again, grinning. "You know, you don't even look like the same girl I met on the bus. Not even a little."

I nod in agreement. "I'm *not*. My whole life has changed since my training." I look at Captain and smile. "To be honest, I never dreamed a Dom could love or care for me so well."

He lifts my chin, gazing into my eyes, and proudly tells everyone in the room, "I enjoy spoiling my pet."

Ena looks at them with a tender look before asking Mr. Gallant, "Should I get the girls now, Husband?"

By the shocked look on Brie's face, it appears she has no idea they have children. While Ena goes to call the girls down, Gallant explains to her, "Our girls are the reason we keep to an informal protocol in our home. What may look informal to an outsider is actually formal between the two of us. We have transformed everyday phrases, titles, and actions so they have personal significance to us."

"That's ingenious," Brie says, glancing at Sir Davis. That prolonged glance makes me wonder if she's hoping they have children in their future.

"It was born out of necessity," Mr. Gallant explains. "Raising two girls, it was important to us to keep our D/s life separate from them."

"Why?" she asks.

"Miss Bennett, we both believe that someone who chooses this lifestyle should do it because it is an inner calling, not simply because they were exposed to it as children. I will be fine if my girls grow up and do not venture into this lifestyle. As long as they find mates who treat them with love and respect, I will be satisfied."

Brie's next question furthers my suspicion about her wanting children. "Is it difficult, living this lifestyle with a young family, Mr. Gallant?"

"It takes careful planning and constant communication. Just like in any marriage, children are a huge commitment. At times, their needs must supersede your own. However, that cannot be allowed to consume the marriage itself. For a D/s relationship—for any relationship, really—the partners must cut out time to care for and support one another. It's essential."

Captain put his arm around me. "Luckily, that is not something the two of us must worry about. Is it, my pet?"

There was a time when knowing I was barren hurt me deeply, but now that no longer holds any power over me. Not with Captain. I grin at my handsome Master, playing with my collar as I answer, "Yes, we have *many* years to play."

I notice Brie lovingly touching her own collar, and I'm reminded of that day she saved me by giving me a business card on the bus.

"Oh, wait!" I blurt out in front of everyone at the dinner table.

Naturally, that causes all of them to look straight at me.

Embarrassed, I mutter to Sir Davis, "I have something for Miss Bennett."

I slide the well-used business card over to Brie—it isn't easy giving it up. This simple card is responsible for changing the course of my life.

Holding my breath, I watch as Brie picks it up with trembling fingers. The look of surprise on her face confirms I've done the right thing.

I apologize. "I know it isn't in the same shape it was when you gave it to me, Brie. You see, I held it many times during my training."

Brie looks down, reading the words out loud:

The Submissive Training Center
25 Years of Excellence

Brie closes her eyes, pressing the business card to her heart. Based on that reaction alone, I couldn't be happier.

"Yeah," I said. "I suspected by the wear on the card when I got it from you that you might want it back."

Brie opens her honey-colored eyes and smiles at me. "It was yours to keep, but I'll admit I'm thrilled to have it in my hands again."

Sir Davis chuckles. "All this sentimentality over a simple business card?"

"This is the one you gave me, Sir."

"Is it now?" he says, taking it from her and looking at it with new interest. "Well, if that's the case, maybe we should frame it."

Brie readily agrees. "That would be lovely, Sir."

He laughs, but when Sir Davis realizes that Brie is serious, he gives her a tender look. Kissing the top of her head, he tells Brie, "If it means that much to you, I'll frame it myself."

As Sir Davis tucks the card away in his wallet, I notice the private wink he gives her. Even though he is more intimidating as a Dom, it is easy to tell his feelings for Brie are as equally strong as Captain's are for me.

I slide my hand under the table and onto Captain's thigh, happy to have returned the card to its original and rightful owner.

Echo

Captain

Echo's decline comes rapidly. One day she is chasing a feisty squirrel that runs in front of her path, and the next, she is curled up in her dog bed, her chin resting on her favorite stuffed animal.

I've known this moment was coming at some point, but this is harder than I thought, and poor Candy is devastated.

"Isn't there something more we can do?" she begs.

"I'm sorry, my pet."

Candy gets on the floor to hug Echo. "I'm not ready to say goodbye…"

"Our one consolation is that she will be reunited with her original master. I'm certain it will be a glorious reunion."

We make her as comfortable as we can, but I know that soon we will have to make the difficult decision of putting her down. Thankfully, however, Echo spares us that.

Early Sunday morning, I head to the kitchen to make a pot of coffee. I hear Echo's heavy breathing and walk over to check on her. Her breath is unusually rapid, and she doesn't move when I call to her.

"Candy, come out here," I say with urgency.

She stumbles out of our bedroom, wiping the sleep from her eyes. "What's up?"

As soon as she sees me kneeling beside Echo, she knows what's wrong. Joining me on the floor, Candy pets her, murmuring, "We love you, Echo."

She wags her tail weakly.

"You've served us well, old pup. It's okay to stop fighting now. You have your master waiting for you," I tell her.

Echo looks up at me longingly as if she has something she wants to say.

I smile as I gather her in my arms. "It was always supposed to end like this. You are well loved, and you will never be forgotten, Echo."

She wags her tail a couple of more times, then her breathing suddenly becomes more labored.

"Should we take her to the vet?" Candy whimpers, tears streaming down her face.

"No, it's too late for that. It happened like this for Troup, too," I explain. "Echo's ready to go home."

We both continue to pet her, sharing our favorite memories, all the while telling her that she's a good dog. There comes a point when the breathing stops for several moments before it starts up again.

I know her body is heroically fighting to continue even as it systematically shuts down.

Echo lifts her head as if she sees someone in the distance and starts wagging her tail.

"Go to him," I tell her.

She slowly lowers her head, her gaze never leaving that exact spot as her breathing comes slower and slower until it stops for the last time.

Candy looks at me questioningly, her eyes swollen and red.

I nod, confirming what she already knows in her heart.

Echo is gone...

I pick her limp body up and head out to the car. "Get a blanket," I tell Candy.

Together, we drive her to the vet, where we arrange for her body to be cremated.

"Would you like us to take a paw print to remember her by?"

I start to say no, but suddenly think back to that note scribbled on Echo's papers at the shelter. "Yes, actually, I would. Thank you."

After several days of research, I discover the address of the couple who surrendered her to the shelter. I want them to know their wishes were honored, and that Echo died well cared for and loved.

I put the paw print plaque, a picture of her with her favorite toy, and a short note into a small shoebox.

Dear Mr. and Mrs. Ryan,

I want you to know that Echo died a peaceful death in my arms. Candy and I enjoyed the time we were given with her and, as you can see from the photo, she was well cared for.

Echo died wagging her tail as if she was happy to move on.

I hope this brings you comfort after the tragic loss of your son.

Sincerely,
Charles

I send the package without a return address, never expecting to hear another word, until Candy notices a short article in the local online news about an old couple who wanted to thank a mystery man named Charles. The article features a message from the parents to him:

You will never know the gift you've given us by taking care of sweet Echo. Our son and Echo were inseparable from the very first day we got her as a pup. When he went off to serve in Afghanistan, she sat by the front door day after day waiting for his return.

You can imagine her joy when he finally came home to us. Unfortunately, he suffered from severe PTSD and Echo was his only comfort. There came a point, however, when even she wasn't enough.

Losing a child is something you never recover from, but you have brought us a sense of closure and peace by caring for Echo in her final days. She will always be connected to our son, so knowing that she passed on wagging her tail has filled us with joy.

Thank you.

Brian and Lori
Proud parents of Second Lieutenant Joseph Ryan

Knowing that Echo's master was not only in the military, but had committed suicide, hits me hard. I remember that first day when I saw her curled up in the kennel…Now, I understand the depths of her sorrow.

I realize what I must do.

Candy and I go to the military cemetery where Joseph is buried. In the dark of night, I open the urn with Echo's ashes and spread it over his grave. I know with certainty this is where she would want to be.

After arriving home, I take out my long list of those who should be remembered. I get out my pen and begin carefully writing his name.

I add Joseph to the list and, alongside his name, I add my personal note.

> Second Lieutenant Joseph Kaleb Ryan, age twenty-seven. Rightfully earned the devotion of Echo, his loyal dog and companion.

Candy comes up behind me. "What is this?"

I look over the numerous pages of my notebook with a profound sense of sorrow. "This is everyone who died under my command. Although Ryan was not one of

157

them, I feel we are connected because of Echo, and I think it's important that he be remembered."

She picks up the notebook and reads through one of the pages, tears coming to her eyes when she reaches the end. "I'm so sorry, Captain."

I take it back from her, looking over their names. Beside each one, I have written a special characteristic or memory associated with the person. I explain to Candy, "After losing so many, I decided none should be forgotten, so I wrote down their name, rank, and the age that they died. But, it was vital they not become just a name. Each of these men had a full life ahead of them. Each one was unique and loved by somebody. I couldn't let their sacrifice be marginalized."

Candy nods, looking back down at the list in reverence.

"After returning to the States, I found the Fourth of July extremely difficult to endure. It was impossible to get any sleep, being tormented by the visions the fireworks incited. For the first two years, I tried to ignore the holiday by going to bed early, hoping to block out the sounds. But the quick fire-bursts and loud explosions mocked the sound of war too closely, and I suffered from panic attacks. Hiding in the dark only invoked hellish nightmares as I listened to the dull thuds and explosions…

"I came to dread the day."

Candy wraps her arms around me. "I can't even imagine."

"When they finally found Grapes' remains and brought him home, I started to feel differently about it.

158

His parents were so quick to forget him, and it made me rage inside. He was a highly respected serviceman and loyal friend who *died* protecting this great country.

"Although the Fourth still triggers memories I want to forget, it is the one day of the year that I see a physical representation of my countrymen banding together in pride as they honor our nation as one.

"I decided then that, rather than fight it, I would embrace the holiday. I found that as long as I could *see* the fireworks, my mind didn't play tricks on me. So, I would sit on my porch, watching the neighbors shoot off their ground fireworks while the cities surrounding LA shot off their professional displays." I snort. "That's not to say it's easy on me. Far from it. As soon as I hear those firecrackers going off a full week before the holiday, the anxiety starts building. And, I know that the night of the Fourth, when I'm finally able to fall asleep, I am going to relive the nightmare of that day over and over again."

I hold up the journal to Candy. "But, as the colorful explosions fill the night sky, I read off my list of those who should be remembered. Over the years, my neighbors began dropping by on the day. Some giving me homemade food to celebrate the holiday." I smile thinking back on it. "One family would even pick out a special firework each year to honor my men, while others insisted on dropping off donations to me in support of wounded soldiers returning home.

"All of it matters to me. Every. Single. Act. Of. Kindness.

"The Fourth has gone from being something I dread,

to becoming the one time each year that I feel connected with my entire community."

Candy's eyes soften, and I can see she understands how significant it is to me. She looks down at my list again, running her finger over the last entry. "Now, Joseph Ryan and Echo will be a part of that remembrance."

The hole left in our lives from Echo's passing takes a toll on both Candy and I. It was surprising, the presence that dog had in our household.

But, that hole is quickly replaced by someone in desperate need the day I get the call from Gallant while I'm at work. Since he has never called me there, I immediately pick up the phone.

"Is something wrong, Gallant?'

"The Submissive Training Center has an emergency situation pertaining to one of our prior graduates. I personally feel you and Candy would be the safest environment for her while she gets the counseling she needs."

"Who are we talking about?"

"Mary Wilson."

I remember the blonde submissive who trained at the same time as Brie Bennett. I've always had a sense she was deeply wounded—even back then.

"Why us?"

"Based on your strict but encouraging guidance as an

officer, as well as Candy's experience with violence at the hands of an abuser, I feel you both will provide her with the help and understanding she needs."

"What's happened? What kind of help are we talking about?"

"Mary has been banned from the commune she's been a part of with Todd Wallace. I won't lie, Captain, it's serious. Lately, she's been gravitating toward a Dom there who closely resembles her abusive father. She's been begging him for increasingly intense impact play. Todd Wallace understands the violence in her past and has forbidden her from continuing, but she refuses to obey him, so he left the commune. Since then, she's completely spiraled out of control, so they felt their only option was to kick her out for her sake and those of the other members."

Even though we have never formally met, I have felt a connection with the girl since the beginning. I have always found her beauty an interesting contrast to my scarred appearance. Despite our drastic physical differences, I have recognized that, like me, she carries a wealth of hidden pain.

"This is *not* something I will consider until I've talked extensively with Candy."

"I would expect no less of you, Captain," Gallant assures me.

When I return home after work, I find Candy studying her textbooks, preparing for her new classes coming up. I hesitate to bring it up with her, not wanting to interfere with her studies or the comfortable situation we have right now.

Candy takes one look at my face and asks, "What's wrong?"

I walk to the couch and motion her to sit beside me. "Nothing is wrong, my pet. However, you and I have been asked to consider a serious responsibility, and I am uncertain if we should even entertain it."

Candy places both of her hands on mine, stating confidently, "Please ask."

As soon as I explain the unhealthy dynamic Mary was seeking at the commune, Candy's response is immediate and forceful. "We *must* help her."

I caress her cheek, wanting to protect this beautiful woman from the potential fallout that taking on this responsibility could bring.

"Captain, although I've never walked in Mary's shoes, I know the devastation that abuse can cause. While you seek to guide her, I can be the shoulder she cries on. However, there's only one way I would agree to this."

"What's that, my pet?" I ask, curious what her stipulation will be.

"I want her to wear your temporary collar."

"*What?*" It's the last thing I expect her to say.

"Hear me out," she pleads.

"Go on."

"It would simply be a collar of protection, without physical attachment, but it would provide two things. For Mary, it will ensure she is cared for and protected. But it will also guard you against unnecessary drama. As your sub, she will be bound to obey you."

I'm struck again by how astute Candy is. "Yes, I can

see the wisdom in your proposal."

"From what you've shared, Mary must be fighting against the abuse of her father by confronting it in this man. But her method is horribly flawed, and now she's lost Faelan because of it."

I frown. "I cannot fault Todd Wallace for leaving. She willfully disobeyed his direct command."

"I agree, Captain. Once Faelan lost his influence over her, leaving was the *only* option he had left."

"Are you certain about taking her on, Candy?" I ask. "Because your well-being is my highest priority. I will do nothing to compromise that."

Laying her head against my shoulder, my sweet pet confesses, "I would not be able to think of anything else if Mary wasn't here with us."

"Does it strike you that we are taking in another Echo—a soul that the world has turned away? Personally, I feel a puppy would be far less complicated."

Candy's eyes sparkle when she answers, "Mary needs us, Captain."

Looking at her, I can't deny a sense of providence. It feels as if we're being led down a path together. "Let's sleep on it to affirm we are still in agreement. But understand this, my pet, any disrespect from her toward you or me will be grounds for dismissal. No matter the severity of her case, I refuse to deal with half-hearted commitments, especially when it profoundly affects our personal lives."

"I completely agree, Captain. I think Mary has to have a hard line drawn or she will continually test it."

I shake my head, my tone severe. "If she even looks

at you the wrong way, she will regret it."

Candy puts her hands on both my cheeks and gives me a tender kiss. "I love how protective you are of me."

I keep my stern expression as we walk toward the bedroom but crack a smile as I pick her up and carry her off to my bed.

"No one torments and teases my little pussy—except me."

Redemption

Candy

S ir Davis brings Mary to us immediately after they
land in LA.

Looking at the poor girl after opening the door, I just
want to cry. Mary looks emotionally battered and lost—
not the confident, sarcastic temptress I have come to
know.

I greet Sir Davis first, feeling deeply grateful that he
has entrusted my Master with her care. "Please come in,
Sir Davis. It's wonderful to see all of you again."

I take Mary's hands in mine and find they are ice
cold. I squeeze them, telling her, "I'm glad to see *you*
especially."

Mary doesn't respond, but I guide her in, along with
Sir Davis and Brie and take them to the sitting room
where Captain is waiting.

He has a collar in his hand.

"Before I allow you into my home, Miss Wilson, I
insist you wear a protection collar. By accepting it, you

are agreeing to follow my house rules, and I am agreeing to care for and protect you. I will only warn you once if you break any of my commands. A second infraction will garner swift punishment, and a third will be cause for dismissal. I do not tolerate any level of disrespect in this home."

The look on Mary's face as she stares at the collar is a mixture of surprise and dread, but she collects herself and asks in a respectful tone, "What are the house rules?"

"You will not leave this house without my permission; you will perform duties to keep this household running smoothly; you are to remain in my presence at all times unless I command otherwise; and you will show the utmost respect to me and my submissive. Do you understand?"

Mary swallows hard before answering, "I do."

"Do you agree to live by these rules?"

Mary glances at Brie momentarily, looking exceedingly anxious, but answers Captain with a "Yes."

"Then kneel at my feet and accept this collar."

My heart races as I watch Mary kneeling before my Master. The expression on Captain's face is one of compassion. He fastens the thin collar around her neck, then puts his hand on her head.

In a commanding voice, he states, "Until the day I remove this collar, you are under my protection and care. You are to address me as Vader for the duration of your stay."

Mary glances up, giving him a surprised look.

I put my hand to my heart, deeply touched. I know

what the title he's given himself means.

Captain explains it to Mary. "My heritage is Dutch. As I am head of this house, and your caretaker, it is fitting you should address me as Father."

I close my eyes, trying to hold back the tears. In taking on the role of a father to Mary, he is claiming power over the unhealthy relationship her biological father had with her.

It's easy to see by the tears now streaming down Mary's face that this has touched on her deepest need. When she's able to find her voice again, Mary answers in a whisper, "Thank you, Vader."

Captain nods to her before speaking to Sir Davis. "Thank you for delivering her to me. My pet and I look forward to aiding in her re-education."

"Dr. Reinstrum will call you soon in order to set up her counseling sessions."

"I've contacted him myself, and it has already been arranged."

Before Brie and Sir Davis leave, Captain gives me a private moment to speak with Brie. I give her a tight hug, so thrilled to see her again. Although I already feel a special bond with her as my rescuer, now that we are both happily collared subs, that bond has grown even deeper.

"Are you okay with this?" Brie asks with concern.

"I'm glad she's come. She needs us."

Brie looks worried when she confesses, "I've never seen her like this before. It's killing me."

"I know, but Captain will see her through to the other side."

Red Phoenix

"She is lucky to have you both." Brie gives me another hug, adding. "*I'm* lucky to have you."

"Mary is in good hands," I assure her, confident in Captain's leadership.

Before Sir Davis leaves with Brie, he asks Mary, "Are you comfortable staying here?"

Wiping the last remaining tears from her eyes, she answers, "Yes. I am, Sir."

Captain places his hand back on Mary's head. "Between my pet and I, I'm confident we can help her to overcome the barriers that hold her back."

I couldn't love Captain any more than I do right now and say proudly, "My Master has a big heart."

With one hand still on Mary's head, Captain cradles my cheek, making a physical statement of my station above Mary. "You are a pleasure to spoil, pet." To emphasize it further, he kisses me, grazing the collar around my neck with his fingers.

Captain looks down at Mary. "Your name will be lief in my home."

"What does it mean, Vader?" she asks, looking as if she expects it's something bad.

"Before I tell you, I want you to tell me what you think it means."

Mary looks down at the floor, a blush of humiliation in her cheeks when she answers meekly, "Lost?"

Captain shakes his head. "I thought you might say something like that. It means 'well-behaved child'. Now, lief, say goodbye to your good friend."

I am left speechless, enchanted by Captain's wisdom. Not only has he established himself as her father figure, he has also given her a name to live up to.

As Mary goes to say goodbye to Brie, it is easy to see she's still a bit shell-shocked by the turn of events. She doesn't know it yet, but being under Captain's care will be the very best thing to have happened to her.

Captain takes his job seriously as her Dom. He gets permission from the Reconnaissance Office to work remotely for the first two weeks Mary stays with us to ensure she follows his rules to the letter.

Their relationship is purely platonic as he re-schools Mary in the art of obedience. He is incredibly strict with her, but he is also equally encouraging. His years as an officer in the Army shine through in his guidance with her.

I'm grateful that Captain still makes time for us as a D/s couple despite Mary's presence. He thinks nothing of petting my hair, kissing me, or having me sit at his feet. He insists on Mary calling me "Miss Cox" at all times, not wanting her to confuse my kindness toward her as weakness.

"You are as important in this re-education as I am," Captain tells me. "I want her to see what respect and love for one another looks like on a practical, daily level. Since she has had neither while growing up, we will provide that example for her."

The first time he feeds me from his plate, Mary rolls her eyes and turns her head. We both see it.

Big mistake.

Captain is on her immediately, barking, "Apologize, lief."

"For what?"

He only glares at her.

It takes Mary a few seconds before she admits her action, and bows her head looking humiliated. "I'm sorry, Vader."

"And?"

She looks up with a confused expression for a moment, then turns to me and bows her head, "I am sorry for rolling my eyes, Miss Cox."

"You are forgiven," I answer in a formal tone, just as Captain has instructed me to do.

"Do not do that again, lief." Captain says. "This is your only warning. Next time, you will be punished severely."

She looks up at him with deep-seated remorse. "I'm sorry. *Please* forgive me."

He puts his hand on her. "I trust you to treat us with respect in thought as well as action.

"Yes, Vader."

After the incident, Mary is thoughtful in her every action around us, and we notice a marked attitude change. It doesn't take long before she begins to feel like a natural part of our family.

I appreciate her sharp wit, and I deeply admire how resilient she is. Truly, Mary is far stronger than people give her credit for, and Captain seems to bring out the best in her.

We are actually unprepared for it when Brie calls to

ask Captain's permission for Mary to tend to Faelan who is struggling after a kidney transplant. Since Brie is being called away to China, she cannot tend him, but doesn't believe Faelan is well enough to be left alone.

Captain is reluctant to grant her request, knowing the progress Mary has made under our care, but he feels strongly that the decision must be Mary's to make, and explains that to Brie before hanging up the phone.

I'm touched when he asks me to join him when he sits down to talk with her.

"As someone who has a vested interest in your welfare, I'm uncertain about this request Brie has made and would therefore advise against it, lief," he states bluntly. "You cannot know what challenges you will find once you get there."

"I understand, Vader," Mary answers. "But I know Brie wouldn't be asking unless the situation is desperate. After everything she and Sir Davis have done for me, I want to return the favor."

"A feeling of obligation is *not* a sound reason to leave here."

Mary glances at me before looking back at Captain. She seems hesitant to confess her real feelings. "Vader…I…still love Faelan. I never thought I would have to chance to see him again."

Captain's expression softens. "Ah, the real reason."

"Although we ended on bad terms, I've never stopped caring about him. If helping Faelan can help Brie as well, going is not even a question for me."

"But by leaving now, you may find yourself back where you started before you came to us."

"Vader, Faelan almost died…I *need* this for me."

As I look at Mary, I can't help thinking about Ethan. Life is not guaranteed.

Having been included in the discussion, I humbly ask him, "May I speak freely, Captain?"

"Certainly, my pet."

"Although the timing of this is not ideal, if we force Mary to stay, it has the potential of ruining what she's gained here with us. This must be a decision she can live with, no matter the consequences that follow."

Captain nods. "While I agree, I still feel it is too soon, lief."

Mary bows her head. "May I be frank, Vader?"

"Naturally."

Still keeping her head down, Mary keeps her tone respectful. "Even though I hold you in the highest regard, if you deny Brie's request that I come, I will leave for Denver anyway."

Captain's concern is easy to read on his face. "I worry for you, lief."

"I won't forget what you've taught me," she vows. "I'll face this like one of your tests and use what I've learned to overcome my old responses."

He looks at Mary tenderly. "Don't lose yourself."

Mary eyes shine with an inner brilliance. "For the first time, I feel ready to open myself to Faelan. I wasn't before, but I am now. I thank you for that."

She glances at me. "I thank *both* of you for being the one thing I've never had…family."

Tears well up in my eyes because I don't want to see her to go. "You'll be severely missed if you leave."

Mary gives me a snorting laugh. "All of my life, I never thought I would *ever* hear those words associated with me."

Captain lifts her chin, setting her gaze on him. "Never doubt that again. You will always be welcome in our home, lief."

Mary swallows hard, looking as if she's about to lose control of her emotions.

I cry the tears she refuses to. She's become like the sister I never had...

Mary wastes no time flying to Denver the very next day. I put on a brave face as I watch her leave, but I'm struggling with the emptiness her departure leaves behind.

Captain wraps his arm around me as we walk back to the car. "This is difficult, I know, but still worth the pain."

I swipe away my tears. "Yes..."

He looks down at me with a rare smile. "I have received a call from Baron. It turns out our dear friend is back in LA and has a secret he'd like to share with us. "Are you game, my pet?"

I can't imagine what Baron's surprise could be, but I'm excited at the prospect of seeing him again.

I take Captain's hand without hesitation and smile up at him. Wherever life takes us, I'm game, as long as he's by my side.

New Vision

Captain

I can tell by the expectant look on Baron's face that he is hiding something significant. He strides up to shake my hand. "Welcome, Captain! You are the first I'm sharing this with."

He grins at Candy, unable to keep his excitement under wraps. "When I discovered it, you two were the first I wanted to tell."

"Enough with all this suspense. Get on with it," I huff good-naturedly.

Baron leads us into his new home, but rushes past the main rooms, leading us down a circular flight of stairs in the back of the house. As we follow him down the steps, Baron tells us, "I thought this feature was oddly charming, but completely pointless."

I can understand why when we reach the bottom of the staircase, because what greets me is a rather unimpressive storage area. Baron tells us, "When I asked the realtor about the circular staircase, he mentioned that the original owner was an extravagant individual who invested in obscure details around the home—hence the decorative stairs that lead to a storage pantry."

I study the walls carefully, noting a difference in pitch at the far end. Baron nods as he watches me. "Yes, you notice it, too." He walks over to the wall and knocks on it. "It has a different feel to it even though it's been made to match the rest of the room exactly. I didn't notice it until my final walkthrough, but it led me to a hunch."

Baron smiles at Candy. "So, you know what I did?"

She shakes her head, her smile growing larger.

"After I signed the papers and the house was officially mine, I bought a sledge hammer."

He glances at Captain. "I won't lie, I had concerns there might be multiple bodies behind that wall. If so, it would render my new purchase a crime scene, but you know what they say about curiosity and the cat…"

He winks at Candy. "I had no choice."

"So, I picked an inconspicuous area easily hidden by boxes, in case I turned out to be wrong about there being a hidden chamber behind this wall."

Baron nods at me, laughing. "Yeah, my heart was seriously pounding when I took that first swing and hit concrete. Talk about a jar to the system. Fuck!"

He shakes his arms as if he can still feel the painful reverberations from the impact. "I almost walked away at that point, but I had a feeling…so, I hit a foot higher."

"And?"

Baron pushes several boxes away from the wall, exposing a grapefruit-sized hole. "You won't believe it."

I raise my eyebrow with a smirk. "How many mummified bodies are in there?"

Grinning, Baron pulls a small flashlight from out of his pocket and kneels beside the hole. "No bodies...but it's something much more interesting."

He shines the light in the hole. I join him on the cement floor and stare inside the dusty cavity. The room looks expansive, and I see a familiar wooden object in the middle. "Is that a St. Andrews Cross?"

"It is!" he announces excitedly. "And I think that's a queening chair sitting beside it."

I gesture for Candy to join us so she can have her own peek. "Do you believe it was a private dungeon?"

Baron shakes his head. "No, it's much too large for that. I'm leaning toward it being a secret club in the forties smack dab in the middle of this uptight LA neighborhood."

Candy sits on her heels after having a look, and giggles. "Not everyone was sleeping in this neighborhood."

"So, explain to me why you haven't demolished the wall already?" I demand with a smirk.

Baron answers by pulling a second sledge hammer out from behind a stack of boxes. "I was just waiting for a friend...or two." He pulls a third one out and gives it to Candy, who sways from the weight of it when he lets go.

As he passes us disposable facemasks and tells us to put them on, he explains, "Nothing is more unsatisfying than to discover something incredible and have no one else to share it with."

He slips his own mask on, and says in a muffled

voice, "Ladies first…"

Candy giggles as she hefts the heavy tool and swings it at the wall. The force barely makes a dent.

"Let me prep it for you," I tell her. I hit the wall with a well-placed strike that has just enough pressure to loosen it, then I instruct her to take another swing. Candy gives it her all this time, and we watch with gratification as chunks of wall crumble to the cement floor.

After that, it becomes a free-for-all as all three of us make short work of the wall. We stand there afterwards, waiting as the dust settles.

Once I deem it safe, I take off my mask and tell him, "You do the honors, Baron."

Candy and I follow behind as he steps into this new part of the house. We begin exploring the abandoned dungeon, finding not only the St. Andrews Cross we've already noted, but also several more of them on the opposite side of the massive room.

Along with the queening chair, there are a variety of spanking benches, stockades, whipping poles, decorative cages, various bondage tables, and even a dual sex swing. Baron walks over to it, fingering the cracked leather. "This has certainly seen better days."

Candy grins. "I can imagine the fun that was had in these…"

"As can I," he agrees, looking the dual swing over with interest as if already contemplating what he would do with it.

"Did you notice the painted walls?" I ask Baron.

"No." He moves away from the swing to brush his

hand against the caked-on dust on the wall. Sweeping the years of dust away reveals a vibrant painting of two submissives on their knees, enthusiastically pleasing their Master.

"A talented artist," Baron states as he stares at the wall.

"Quite stimulating," I agree, feeling a surge of desire as I examine the erotic painting. I glance at Candy, imagining the things I want to do to her when we return home.

"Do you think this was a private club for the elite?" Candy asks Baron.

"It sure as hell looks like it to me. I'm going to start researching the original owner and see what I can find out about the man."

I look around the enormous dungeon, wondering what's to become of it. "What do you plan to do with this?"

That's when I get an answer I'm not expecting.

"All this equipment shouldn't go to waste. And this is an ideal setup…" Baron looks around at all the tools and equipment. "I think I have the perfect use for it, but it would have to include both of you."

I am not ignorant of the fact Baron is attracted to Candy, but I have no interest in becoming a threesome. Before I can reply, he states, "Captain, you and I are of a similar bent. I saw it in how you handled Liege, and now with Mary."

Candy shoots a surprised glance at me, and I groan inside. Baron has no idea that I've never told her about my encounter with Liege. I ignore her questioning gaze, wanting to discuss it with her later, in private.

"What are you envisioning, Baron?"

"You know I case the BDSM clubs, looking to protect subs from wannabes, but I see the greater need. A one-night rescue isn't always enough. There are some subs who have been damaged by the unhealthy power exchanges they've suffered, and they need guidance. The three of us could provide that for them in a safe environment. Not only to overcome their past, but to also regain their power as individuals."

"And how would we accomplish that?" I ask, intrigued.

Baron smiles when he answers. "In much the same way as the Submissive Training Center—through instruction. However, it will be at a much slower and more limited capacity."

He turns to Candy. "That's why your input would be invaluable for these submissives. Both Captain and I can explain and demonstrate the dynamics of a healthy BDSM scene as Dominants, but you add the perspective of a submissive and can empathize with their struggles in overcoming past abuse." His voice becomes somber when he tells her, "Captain and I can show them what to expect in a Dominant but you, Candy, can act as their guiding light."

I have a concern, based on the basic structure of the program he's shared with us. "When you say it would be modeled after the Training Center, are you meaning the practicums, as well? Because—"

Baron holds up his hand. "No, Captain. This is about guidance, not practice. We want them to become reacquainted with the common BDSM tools and equipment in a positive and nonthreatening environment. Our program would provide a safe place for them to ask questions, observe, and test the tools and equipment for themselves. What they choose to do afterward is entirely up to them."

"This sounds amazing!" Candy exclaims.

"But how would it be funded?" I ask, wanting to know the logistics before committing to anything.

"It would take place after business hours, and there would be no compensation for your time. However, I would provide this place and seek out donations from the BDSM community to help support our efforts."

Candy looks at me hopefully, but I appreciate that she isn't putting me on the spot by asking for my answer now, in front of Baron.

What she doesn't know, however, is that I have already made up my mind. "If Candy is agreeable, I would be honored to join you in this endeavor."

Baron looks to Candy, who nods her head vigorously. "You couldn't stop me!"

Holding out his hand to me, Baron shakes it firmly. "To the beginnings of a productive partnership, Captain."

The glint in his eyes speaks to the level of passion he feels about this project, and I am emboldened by it.

When Baron lets go of my hand, he shakes Candy's next. "The three of us are going to change lives," he states.

"I know," Candy answers confidently.

Looking around the space, Baron suddenly stops for a moment and closes his eyes. A heavy silence falls over the area. When he opens them again, he explains, "I felt the breath of Adrianna's presence just now." Baron's smiles broadens. "I'll take it as her blessing."

I stand there, looking at the three of us—each seeking to find meaning after suffering tragic losses. Our need for purpose binds us together in ways others will never understand.

"Now comes the hard part," Baron states, looking over all the dusty equipment. "It's our solemn duty to test out each and every piece of furniture here for quality assurance."

He looks at me with a smirk. "Don't you agree, Captain?"

On the way home, the question that has been burning in Candy's heart finally finds its voice.

With a tremble in her voice, she asks, "Captain, what did Baron mean when he said that you handled Liege?"

I reach over and stroke Candy's cheek as I keep my eye on the road. "I didn't do it for you, my pet. I did it strictly for me."

"Did what?" she cries.

Frowning, I turn to her briefly to answer. "I simply went there to collect all his video tapes, and to warn him never to attempt it again."

Candy looks at me warily. "Why don't I believe you?"

"I didn't hurt him," I growl. "I just scared the bastard."

Candy shakes her head slowly, looking even more upset. "Why didn't you tell me?"

"The two of us were not a couple at the time, so I felt no reason to burden you with it."

"Was the plan to always keep it a secret from me, then?"

"Candy, you told me never to say his name again— that you couldn't stand thinking about him, even for a second. I simply made sure you never had to."

She looks at me sideways. "But Liege is still alive, right?"

"Of course. Unless he's killed himself out of his own sheer stupidity, which would be no fault of mine."

"Captain, you shouldn't have gone there," she says, looking troubled.

I purposely hold back mentioning the fact that he had another girl captive in his apartment when I arrived. I don't want Candy focusing another second of her life on that fucker. "I haven't been to see him again," I assure her.

What I don't say is that I've been checking up on him regularly with my spyware to ensure he doesn't hurt another living soul.

Candy's troubled expression slowly relaxes, and I finally see a speck of a smile emerging. "Although it makes me sick to think about you taking that risk...I do appreciate your protective nature, Captain."

"I would do anything to protect you."

"Yes, that's exactly what I'm afraid of."

I shake my head. "Don't be. I would never risk my life needlessly. You and I have too much to live for."

Old Fears

Candy

During the day, I take my marketing classes, looking like any other college student on campus. At night, however, I join Captain and Baron as we plan out how to help emotionally scarred submissives regain their power and confidence.

As much as I enjoy the creativity and research involved in marketing, what the three of us are planning to do with this program is far more exciting to me.

To help someone slowly open up and trust again who has been crushed by physical violence or mental abuse, is life changing. I know Baron and Captain have the needed compassion to inspire that trust, as well as the dominance to push each individual to grow further.

This secret club under Baron's house will be transformed into a safe haven for the broken women and men in our BDSM community—a place where they will be fully accepted right where they are emotionally as they find their way back to who they truly want to be.

The three of us feel strongly that Baron and Captain cannot take on the roles as temporary Dominants, even in a severely limited capacity. Emotional ties could form that would hinder a submissive's progress.

Baron suggests reaching out to Sir Thane Davis to see if he and Brie would have any interest in joining our team as a couple. With his extensive knowledge and experience, along with their strong D/s dynamic, they could provide needed instruction while remaining emotionally distant from those they are working with.

We both agree, so Baron arranges for Sir Davis to call once they return from their honeymoon.

Captain gets the call early in the morning. I hold my breath as I listen to the one-sided conversation, anxious to learn what Sir Davis has to say.

"How does next Wednesday at noon work, after your return?"

There's a momentary pause before Captain replies, "Excellent. We are looking forward to sharing our plans with you."

Another short pause and he chuckles. "Yes, Baron has been chomping at the bit to tell you for a while now."

Captain's look of surprise alarms me, until I hear him laugh. "I must admit I never saw you as a doting husband but, then again, you never take on any job without giving it your full attention."

My heart melts when he says that about Sir Davis. I love knowing that Brie is married to a Dominant who isn't afraid to love his wife so well.

"Think nothing of it. If such a simple request will

provide you peace of mind while you travel this week, we'll be happy to do it. Candy and I can even visit her, if you'd like."

I perk up, excited by the prospect of seeing Brie for a social visit.

"I'll be sure to ask. Safe travels, Sir Davis. I look forward to speaking to you next week."

After hanging up the phone, I ask, "How did he seem?"

"Like a man who doesn't want to leave his new wife," he says, chuckling to himself.

"About our meeting with him?"

"He definitely seemed interested. I have a good feeling about it, although the fact that Brie is expecting may complicate things for us."

I giggle. "I can't believe she got pregnant that fast! They didn't even get to enjoy being newlyweds."

"I'm certain it was strategic on Davis's part. Better to be a father at his age than to wait and be one at mine."

I wrap my arms around him joyfully. "Well, that's something you and I don't have to concern ourselves with."

He kisses the tip of my nose. "I have a gift for you, kitten…"

I purr happily. "You do?"

"Yes. You will find it in my closet. There is a pink bow on the box."

I run to the closet, my heart swelling when I see the box with the pink bow sitting on the shelf. I pick it up and carry it back to him, grinning excitedly.

"You have kept up on your studies while working

every night with both Baron and I on this project. I think it's high time I spoil my kitten."

I bite my bottom lip. Captain has taken on the household responsibilities in order to allow me time to devote to my courses. Really, I should be the one spoiling him...and I definitely plan to tonight.

At his insistence, I untie the satin bow and pull off the lid. I see the gifts have been packed in layers, the top one being a golden pet bowl engraved with my name.

"I love it!" I cry, picking it up to admire the shiny bowl.

"I like seeing you drink out of pretty things," he says in a sensual tone.

I lift a pink layer of paper to reveal a fuzzy pair of pink cat ears with stylish maroon tips. I hold it out to him and close my eyes as he places it on my head.

"Adorable," he says with a wink.

I lift the next layer of paper and find a golden plate with rhinestones set around the edge.

"For when I share a meal with you," he says in a gruff voice.

Already I'm anticipating the evening ahead and sigh with contentment as I lift the final layer. I let out a little gasp when I see it.

"Do you like it?"

I stare at the furry kitten tail attached to a gold butt plug. My eyes widen as I pick up the soft faux fur tail and notice it's decorated with a pink bow and jewel tied at its base.

My heart starts to race, knowing tonight will be our first time exploring anal play together.

"I think it's beautiful," I tell him, smiling shyly. "I can't wait to wear it."

Captain nods, pleased at my reaction.

He instructs me to put the items back in the box for later, but to leave the kitten ears on my head. I spend the afternoon finishing my research paper.

My pussy is wet the entire time just thinking about the night's events ahead.

I glance at him while I work, and the butterflies start up again. Leave it to Captain to make anal play something pretty and romantic...

At six, Captain tells me to close my books and turn on the news while the two of us start preparing dinner together. I love our time in the kitchen when we choose a new recipe to try. Just as I'm laying out the ingredients for our meal, I hear Captain command, "Stop."

I look up to see him staring intently at the television. I turn my head to see a fiery explosion as a large jumbo jet crashes to the ground.

I cover my mouth in horror as it disintegrates before my eyes. As the news replays the video, I hear the commentator say the plane had just taken off from LAX, headed for Dubai.

"Oh, my God, did that just happen here?" I ask Captain.

"Put everything away," he orders in a calm voice.

Despite the even sound of his tone, I know something is horribly wrong. "What is it?"

He turns to me. "Sir Davis was on that plane."

"No!" I cry in horror as I look back at the TV screen and watch again as the plane explodes as it crashes to the ground.

I pull off my kitten ears and lay them on the counter, a sick feeling growing in my stomach. As I put away the ingredients, I listen as Captain talks on the phone, asking for information about Sir Davis.

It doesn't seem real…this can't be real.

"Come, I have information for Mrs. Davis," Captain tells me.

I go to grab my purse, but drop it, my whole body numb from shock. Captain picks it up and gently takes my arm, guiding me to the car.

On the drive over, he tells me, "Brie is going to need your strength right now. You can't give in to your own emotions or fears. You are there solely as her friend and support. This is about getting her through this event intact."

I nod, but my heart and head are reeling as the vision of that horrifying plane crash replays in my mind. "Do you think he survived?" I whisper.

"There are survivors," Captain answers.

I close my eyes, holding on to that hope.

He has to be alive…

I struggle to breathe while Captain knocks on Brie's door. My heart feels like it's going to break when she swings the door wide, greeting us with a bright smile.

She doesn't know…

"Hey, you guys! What an unexpected surprise."

My heart stops beating for a moment, knowing he has to tell her. I look at Brie knowing her whole world is about to be torn apart.

Brie doesn't understand why we're acting oddly and

grimaces, then laughs. "Umm…forget I said anything about Mary. She's going to kill me if she knows I talked to you."

"Brie, I think you should sit down," I tell her, leading her toward the couch.

She looks at me strangely, and then stares at Captain. "What's this about? You guys are starting to scare me."

Captain's voice is calm and exact. "We have some disturbing news, but I need you to focus on what I am about to say."

Brie's face drains of all color. I grab her hand, willing my strength into her as Captain explains, "There's been a plane crash at LAX. I've been able to confirm that Sir Davis was on that flight."

Brie's whole body begins to shake, and I squeeze her hand tighter.

"Brianna," he states in a firm voice. "There *are* survivors. Although I can't confirm he is one of them, *that* is what you must focus on right now."

Captain looks at me, before telling her, "First, we need you to get dressed. Then, I'll drive you to the hospital that is receiving survivors."

I understand my role and guide Brie down the hallway to help her change. I keep saying over and over, "He's alive, Brie. I'm sure of it…"

Maybe if I say it enough, it will make it true.

As I get her ready, I silently pray that Brie will not have to suffer the same fate I did with Ethan.

I bring her out to Captain, keeping up a brave face when he tells her, "I know this is hard—the not knowing—but you must be strong. There is no point entertaining what-ifs until you know the truth about the situation. Even then, no matter what the news, Sir Davis would expect you to be courageous for the health of the baby."

The baby...

I look down at her stomach, and my gut twists. The baby may be Brie's last tie to Sir.

Captain is an incredible pillar of strength the entire night, keeping Brie focused as we search the hospital for Sir Davis. When we've searched them all without finding him, he convinces Brie that it's time to go to the morgue.

"I can't..." Brie whimpers to him.

"You will. Sir Davis deserves no less," he tells her.

I admire how strong Brie is in that moment, facing the one thing I never could have with Ethan. Thankfully, fate has heard my prayers for her. Before we ever make it to the morgue, we get the call that there is a second group of survivors.

In that group, Brie finds Sir Davis. He's unconscious and his body is broken—but he is alive!

As Captain and I sit in the waiting room, I reverently take his hand and press it against my cheek. "You were amazing."

He shakes his head.

"No, you were, Captain. You carried the weight of this on your shoulders the entire night. You were the strength Brie desperately needed."

He looks down for several moments before turning his head toward me. I'm hit by the emotional toll this evening has taken on him. Without even thinking, I crawl into his lap and embrace my strong warrior.

"I can't handle losing another one. I can't..." he confesses in a ragged voice.

I hold him even tighter, realizing how close to the edge he is. I silently lift Sir Davis up in prayer, for not only Brie's sake, but also our own.

Meeting Destiny

Captain

I can feel it coming.

It started with Sir Davis' accident several month ago, and the sensation has intensified ever since. It feels as if everything is converging, leading me down a particular path, and I am powerless to stop it.

I've heard rumors that Brie has a stalker bent on hurting her. It's confirmed by the fact that Anderson, Nosaka and Durov have come to her aid.

However, it isn't until Rytsar Durov is captured and beaten by Russian thugs on a surveillance tape broadcasted all over national TV that I know my time has come.

I look at Candy with a sense of nostalgia now, cherishing the simple things about her—the flirtatious way she tilts her head, those big, round doe-like eyes, and her kittenish smile that never ceases to move me.

When I get word that Davis is looking for people to form a rescue team, I know I am destined to be a part of that mission. Although I am not close friends with Durov, he plays an important role in the BDSM community and I have always admired his work against human trafficking.

I hate that I must have this conversation with Candy. And, as much as I want to put it off, I love her too much to leave her in the dark.

"Candy."

She looks up from her studies. I note the dark circles under her eyes. She hasn't been able to think about anything else since seeing the surveillance footage of an unconscious Durov being dragged away. This attack hit too close to home for any of us to ignore, but this affects my sweet Candy more than most because of her sensitive spirit.

"We need to talk, my pet."

With a look of apprehension, she slowly closes her textbook. "What is it?"

I pat the area next to me on the couch. "I need to talk to you about what's happened to Durov."

She suddenly looks ill. "I can't stop thinking about it. Poor Rytsar. Poor Brie. I know how close they are." Her voice breaks when she adds, "It was just so terrible to watch, and no one's seen or heard from him since."

I put an arm around her when she sits down beside me. "Davis is gathering a small group to fly to Russia and attempt a rescue mission."

Her eyes widen with fear when she realizes what I am about to say. "No, Captain…"

"As much as I long to stay here with you, my pet, I know what needs to be done and I am the man to do it."

She grabs on to me. "Those men are ruthless killers. They would think nothing of shooting you and leaving you to die."

I nod in agreement. "You're absolutely right, which is why my military background necessitates I be part of this rescue mission."

"But I can't let you go," she whimpers, holding me tighter.

I look down at her with compassion, having gone through all the emotions she is going through now. Denial, anger, and then, finally…acceptance. I do not have a choice in this matter, and I explain why to her.

"Candy, whoever goes on this mission *will* die if I do not join them. Not one who has offered to go has the skills and expertise needed for the operation. To stay behind when I know their fate is too much for me to bear as a man."

"But, Captain, we have everything to live for—you and me!" she cries, tears welling up in her eyes.

"I'll do everything in my power to return to you."

She buries her head in my chest. "I don't want you to go to Russia."

"But you understand why I must."

She says nothing for several moments, but eventually mutters into my chest, "Yes…"

I hold her closer, letting my own tears fall. I know there's a real chance I may not make it back to her—and I'm not ready to lose Candy.

However, I feel in my bones that I am the one to lead this mission.

After I allow us a moment to feel the fear for what's

ahead, I clear my throat and bring up a topic I know will be very hard for her to hear. I wipe her tears away and smile tenderly at her. "There is something you and I must agree on."

"What's that?" she asks, miserably.

"I cannot leave unless I know you will be well cared for."

She looks at me in shock. "What are you saying?"

"If the worst happens, I need to know you will be okay both emotionally and physically."

"Okay? How could I ever be okay?" she exclaims.

"I misspoke." I pet her hair as I try again. "I meant that you would have a Dom to protect and care for you in the event I do not return."

She shakes her head, tears streaming down her face.

"I know this is difficult, but it's essential I have that peace of mind, my pet. I cannot worry about you if I hope to succeed in this mission."

She continues to shake her head. "No, Captain...no..."

I nod, my voice choking up with emotion when I confess, "I need this for me. I vowed I would always care for you. I can't abide the thought of my beautiful girl struggling alone."

Candy throws her arms around me, sobbing. I hold myself upright, not giving in to the emotions that threaten to overwhelm me.

"I need a name. A Dom you trust to carry you through the hardships you would face."

"I can't believe we're talking about this," she whimpers.

I cradle her chin, gazing into her eyes. "I love you. I will do everything in my power to return to you, but I need you to do this for me. Please."

She smashes her face against my chest again, nodding her head. I give her time to respond, knowing how difficult this is for her because of how difficult it is for me.

Finally, she pulls away, wiping her cheeks with her hands. With red-rimmed eyes, she meets my gaze. "If I must choose for your sake, then I choose Baron."

I smile, nodding. "It is the choice I would make for you as well."

Candy shakes her head. "But I don't want another Dom."

I envelop her in my arms. "I promise I will move heaven and Earth to make it back to you, my love."

She slowly begins to relax in my arms. "I believe you, but I don't trust fate."

I snort. "Fate has not been kind in the past."

She looks up at me. "I have to believe we were brought together for a purpose—that love will win out in the end."

"Agreed, my pet. We will look back on this moment, knowing how much courage it took for us to do this, and we will be encouraged by it in the future."

Candy caresses my scarred cheek. "You've always been the courageous one. Now, I must be brave, too."

"Thank you." I close my eye, concentrating on the rhythm of her heartbeat. Truly, of everything I've done since returning home, this is by far the hardest I've had to face. If I did not have her support, I would struggle to leave.

"The volunteers meet tonight with Davis. He'll decide the final team. I will speak to Baron then."

She cuddles against me. "I want you to find Rytsar alive and come back quickly. That is my only prayer until I see this beautiful face again."

I nuzzle her. "I will be offering up the same prayer, my pet."

I walk into Davis's hospital room along with Marquis Gray. He will not be part of the rescue team, but has come in support. I suspect he's involved in some way with protecting Brie from the stalker.

Brie and Todd Wallace are already there, standing on the other side of Sir Davis's hospital bed.

It appears that Davis is surprised to see Marquis there. "I specifically instructed Wallace to leave you out of this."

"It wasn't Mr. Wallace who called me," Marquis answers, glancing at me.

I give Davis a curt nod, gratified to see him alive and recovering. "Let me just say what a blessing it is to see you awake."

He grasps my hand, his grip weak and shaky. Davis has a long road of rehabilitation ahead, but I see the fire in his eyes and trust he will recover.

"Captain, Brie told me you were instrumental in bringing her to my bedside after the crash. She claims she would not have survived the ordeal without you."

I glance at Brie. "Your wife exaggerates. She is strong in her own right."

"Still, you made that difficult time easier for her."

"I did nothing more than you would have, Sir Davis," I assure him.

Baron is the next to arrive. I can't help staring at him as he interacts with Davis. The man has a solid character, one worthy of Candy.

"I'm glad to see you here, but what about Candy? This is too dangerous to take the risk. That girl needs you," Baron tells me, clearly concerned.

I shake my head. "This is far too important for me to stay away."

I'm surprised to see Boa, the brawny submissive enter the room. The support of this community toward one of their own is truly inspiring to witness. I am proud to be included among them.

Davis tells Boa, "While I'm glad to see you, I have to admit I'm surprised."

Boa firmly shakes his hand. "Mistress and I had a long discussion when we heard from Captain about what was going on here tonight. If I can be of service, I'm willing to offer myself with my Mistress' full support."

Davis looks at me, and then back at Boa. "I'm moved that all of you have come. However, I do not want to break up partnerships, as this will be a dangerous undertaking."

"The offer still stands, Sir Davis," Boa states as Anderson enters the room with a flourish, swinging his cowboy hat overhead.

"Let's go save that Russian bastard!" Anderson proclaims.

Davis quickly shoots down his offer. "I'm afraid you're not going."

Anderson looks at him in surprise. "Why?"

"You are…" Davis begins.

"A gimp," Wallace finishes with a smirk.

Anderson flashes Wallace a mocking grin. After a little back and forth, Davis tells Anderson the simple truth. "You're not fully recovered from your broken leg and we can't compromise your safety or those that you would work alongside of."

Anderson appears upset, but attempts to laughs it off as he stares at Wallace. "I truly hate that Wolfie gets to have all the fun." He turns his attention back on Davis, "But you know I'll support you however you need me."

The room grows quiet when Ms. Clark makes her appearance. I am shocked to see her, knowing the long and complicated history she has with Durov. After an emotional reunion with Davis, she asks, "So, when do we leave?"

"Not so fast, Samantha," Davis tells her. "This is a covert operation that only requires three people."

I look at those represented in the room and it's not a surprise that I'm the oldest here. As I glance at each young face, I'm struck by how many years they still have ahead of them and I feel the overpowering need to protect those futures.

I was unsuccessful with my own men, but I will not fail my friends now.

"Who here speaks Russian?" Davis asks.

Although I have some basic vocabulary, I am far from proficient. Only Clark raises her hand.

"By default, you will be going," Davis announces. He then informs the rest of us, "You should all know I have already requested that Mr. Wallace join the rescue effort."

My heart begins to race as I look at Mistress Clark and the boy, Wallace. They are no match against the Koslov Brothers. Without a solid strategy in place, they will die before they ever make it to the compound.

Davis tells us, "I have already eliminated Boa from the list. I do not want Mistress Lou to be without her favorite sub."

Boa accepts his dismissal graciously. "So be it, Sir Davis. I will still assist in any way you need."

Davis tells Marquis, "As you are already aware, you will not be involved in this rescue mission. Protect Celestia and the school. That will be your service in this operation."

Marquis nods. "As Mr. Wallace has been recruited to help in the rescue mission, I will take care of all other matters that require your attention."

His reply to Davis solidifies my suspicions about his involvement concerning the stalker. I trust he will be able to bring resolution to the problem for both Brie and Sir Davis's sake.

"That just leaves me and my friend Captain," Baron states, smiling at me.

"Captain, like Boa, you have a mate and should not abandon her," Davis tells me.

"I disagree," I reply. "Of all of us present, I am the

only one who understands covert operations. The Koslov brothers are an organized band of men every bit as dangerous as those factions I fought in the war. I am the *only* choice."

"What about Candy?" Davis protests.

"She and I have already discussed this. I am but one old man. Strategically, it makes no sense to sacrifice Baron when I can ensure our success."

"I can't let you do that," Baron declares. "Candy needs you."

I face Baron, fighting to keep my voice even and calm when I tell him, "Candy has asked that you become her Master, should I not return from this mission."

I hear the others gasp around me.

Davis cries, "No! Durov would never accept such a sacrifice."

I look at Baron and ask formally, "Would you take my sub as your own, should I perish?"

Baron's jaw goes slack. "Don't ask this of me."

"Why? You do not want her?"

"No, it is not that. I don't want to lose you, my friend."

I am deeply affected by his sincerity and put my hand on his shoulder. "There is no one else I would want to care for my pet. She is very precious to me."

Baron shakes his head, looking bereft, but he still gives me the answer I need to hear. "I would be honored to take Candy as my own."

I squeeze his shoulder before letting go. He's given me the peace of mind I need to move forward. Turning to Davis, I announce, "Then, it is settled. You have your team. When do we depart?"

Davis stares at us in silence. With great effort, he grabs the rails of the bed and forces himself into an upright position. "Thank you for your friendship, your courage, and your selfless hearts. I won't forget this." His voice falters as he lays back down, tears of gratitude in his eyes.

I take over, not wanting to waste another second. "We need nonessentials to leave so we can formulate our strategy and execute it quickly and efficiently."

My plan is to return to Candy as fast as humanly possible—with all of us accounted for.

Baron, Marquis, Anderson, and Boa shake hands with those of us who are going. It is a solemn moment because we understand that one or more of us might not make it back.

I clasp Baron's shoulder as I shake his hand. Leaning in, I whisper, "She'll need you by her side in the weeks ahead."

He looks me in the eye. "She and I will concentrate our energy on our mutual project while we wait for your return."

There are no other words left to say but "Thank you, Baron."

My beautiful girl keeps up a brave face as we wait to board the plane for Russia. There are no tears when I bend down to kiss her goodbye.

"I know you are the man to lead this mission and bring Rytsar back home," she states confidently. "I love you, Captain."

I nod, grateful she understands. "I will not rest until I return to you."

"I'm counting on that."

"It is difficult to leave your side," I tell her, caressing her cheek.

She looks up at me with those doe-like eyes. "Don't worry about me. I'll be waiting with bells on when you come home."

I smile, imagining her in nothing but her belled collar. She has no idea what her support means to me at this moment. I will not let her down.

Giving Candy one more kiss, I savor the softness of her lips before we part. God knows I don't want to leave her.

I turn and start walking toward the plane, not allowing myself to look back when I hear her say, "God speed, Captain."

With Davis's help, we have negotiated a ransom, but he warns us that the Koslov brothers do not seem happy about the arrangement. I accelerate our plans for extraction, not wanting the brothers to change their minds.

When we reach their isolated compound in Siberia, the three of us are accosted and beaten, leaving me to wonder if we're already too late.

Knowing the unstable nature of the two brothers, I've instructed my team that we are not to fight back. Instead, the plan is to let Clark take the lead. As a female, the two brothers will assume authority over her and think less of Wallace and me for letting her lord over us. It allows us to hide behind a position of perceived weakness as we scope out the environment.

All three of us, bloodied by the "welcome party" before, are dragged in front of the two brothers and thrown to the floor. One look at Durov, who is tied to a chair beside the two men, and I know time has run out. He has been starved and beaten to the point that he is hardly recognizable or coherent.

I glance at Clark, who, to her credit, keeps a stoic face as she stares hard at Durov—the man she has risked everything for.

Gavriil, the oldest of the brothers, asks Durov tauntingly, "Do they seem familiar to you, worm?"

Durov grunts angrily in answer, turning his head from us. Even in his compromised condition, he still reasons out what is happening and responds accordingly.

Although the tension in the room is high, I hold out hope that my plan will work.

"American fools," Gavriil states. He places his boot on Clark's back and leans down, resting the barrel of his gun against her temple. "What would you do, worm, if I shot her right now?"

Stas stares intently at her and suddenly clears his throat to get Gavriil's attention.

Something passes between them, because Gavriil slowly removes his foot and smiles down at Clark.

"Wait...is this the infamous Mistress Clark? The woman who humiliated Durov in every way a man can be? Stas is quite the admirer of yours." He chuckles as he holds out his hand to her. "My sincerest apologies, Mistress."

The three of us are stunned by the sudden change in Gavriil's tone—Clark most of all. She takes his hand and stands up slowly with an air of pride about her. "I am one and the same," she answers, her voice cold with disdain.

Gavriil turns to Rytsar in amusement. "These heathens aren't here for your rescue, after all..."

The older brother is entertained by the thought that Clark has come to exact her own revenge on Durov. It gives us leverage we're not expecting, and she plays upon it brilliantly. "My colleagues and I are here on behalf of Vlad Durov. The man you made the offer to," she says. "But he will be extremely unhappy when he finds out the manner in which I, his representative, have been treated."

Gavriil scoffs. "Vlad would *never* align himself with a woman."

All the men in the room chuckle.

"Rest assured, I *am* here on Vlad's behalf and have proof." She nods toward the door. "Except one of your men stole the timepiece I was instructed to give you."

Gavriil sends Stas to get the timepiece, and while he waits, he flirts with the Mistress. "You're quite a looker. While I'm no bitch like Durov, I wouldn't mind showing you a taste of Russian hospitality." He moves in close and growls lustfully. "Let me show you what a real man does with American pussy."

Clark looks at him with contempt. "I would break every bone in your body if you dared to try." She glances down at Wallace and me with a superior look. "Just ask my men."

"Ah…" Gavriil laughs at us. "So these are *your* men, not the other way around."

"Of course not. I bow to no man."

He takes that as a sexual challenge and moves closer, stating with a seductive undertone, "I bet I could make you bow."

Stas returns with the item. But, for some odd reason, Gavriil ignores him. I sense there is a rift between the two and trust we can use it to our advantage.

Strolling over to Rytsar, Gavriil laughs as he points to Clark. "Tell me, worm. How does it feel to have your balls crushed in her hands?" His laughter fills the room.

Clark has taken the older brothers' defenses down with her banter and practically has him eating out of her hand.

"Let's finish this up, shall we?" she replies in a bored voice. Looking at the two of us, Clark commands us to stand up.

I slowly get to my feet, still wary of the two men.

Gavriil tells Stas, "Check the account to verify the transfer has been made by Vlad."

Stas dutifully leaves the room again. I've noticed he has remained silent this entire time and does not seem to be mesmerized by Clark the way Gavriil is. No, his attention has remained focused solely on Durov. Something about that does *not* sit right…

"The deal is done, then," Gavriil announces when

Stas returns nodding his head, indicating the money has been transferred.

Clark orders us to untie Durov and adds as an after-thought, "No need to be gentle with the merchandise."

I quickly begin untying Rytsar's bonds, but Stas waves Gavriil over and whispers in his ear.

I get a sinking feeling in my gut. Something bad is about to go down.

"Wait," Gavriil orders. "Stas has brought up an excellent point. It is not right that Durov leave here without a sacrifice. He killed a member of our family. There must be restitution."

"Isn't that what the ransom is for?" Clark insists.

"No, an attack on the Koslovs as grievous as this requires a physical restitution be made. Something we can give to the family."

"Meaning?" she asks, her voice cold as ice.

"An eye for an eye."

My stomach twists in a knot.

"He will not leave until we have a sacrifice, and we will not accept it from the worm himself." Gavriil smiles at Wallace and me. "Which means it must come from one of you."

Durov growls, struggling violently in his bonds, but they completely ignore him as Stas produces a large knife and moves toward us. I purposely shift my feet to garner the man's attention. I need to be the one, not Wallace—he's still a boy.

I am the leader of this mission and I will make the sacrifice willingly.

Stas wears a crazy, closed-mouth grin as he taps the

knife against the leather patch covering my eye. I don't move a muscle as he slowly repositions the blade, setting the tip against the edge of my right eye.

I gaze straight into Stas's eyes, unafraid, but one thought runs through my head.

I will never see Candy's face again...

I refuse to flinch as he begins pressing the knife into the soft tissue of my eye. Giving up my sight to ensure the entire party gets out alive is worth this price.

"I'll do it," I hear Wallace say beside me.

I groan when Stas moves away and walks over to Wallace, a crazy laugh escaping his lips as he does so.

Staring deep into those blue eyes, he looks from one to the other, as if trying to decide which one to take. Clark steps between them and warns him, "No one hurts my men."

But Stas is legitimately insane, and turns the blade on her.

Gavriil growls, "Do *not* touch her."

The tension rises to dangerous levels as the two brothers face off—one with a gun, the other with a blade—while their henchmen circle around them nervously.

Fuck!

It seems we're going to have to take them all down or be caught in the crossfire.

Wallace states loudly, "The offer has been made and I stand behind it."

Gavriil turns to him with a look of relief. "You will act as the worm's payment, *da*?"

"Yes," Wallace answers firmly.

As he sits down, the reality of what is about to happen settles over the group. Both Clark and I attempt to stop him, but several henchmen subdue us, forcing us to watch as Stas digs out Wallace's eye and holds it up for everyone to see.

The silence in the room afterward is chilling; the only sound is Wallace's labored breathing.

My admiration for Wallace knows no bounds, and I will forever be in his debt for the sacrifice he has made for the team. However, I now have a second mission before I leave Russia—Stas and Gavriil must die.

I make quick work of Durov's bindings and walk Wallace out myself, pressing my shirt against his eye socket.

I cannot believe we leave the compound unharassed. I don't trust it, and keep watch, expecting an ambush at any second as we head toward the helicopter waiting for us.

There is an unexpected delay when Durov insists on waiting for a stray dog he has named *Glupyy* or "Foolish". He refuses to leave without the animal. Although it is an unwanted risk, I understand the connection between a man and his dog. Thankfully, for all of us, the mutt makes a beeline for the Russian and our entire party gets onto the copter without incident.

It isn't until we are out of range and headed to Moscow that I finally let my guard down. Both Durov and Wallace need immediate medical attention, but we have accomplished our objective. Rytsar Durov has been liberated and every member of the team is still alive.

I came into this mission thinking I would be the one

to save them, but Wallace has proven himself a true soldier. I will send him home to recover in the States while the three of us—Clark, Rytsar and myself—stay behind to neutralize the threat.

The Koslov brothers have proven themselves far too unstable and dangerous to ignore.

My return to Candy must be postponed for a little while longer.

Understanding

Candy

As I watch Captain get on the plane, I know I have a choice to make. I can give in to my fear and the pain his leaving is causing, or I can move forward each day we are separated with the expectation of success.

He *will* be successful in his mission.

Rytsar will come home—they all will—and Captain will finally know peace.

That is my vision and the hope I hold onto.

While I wait, I finish the last of my college courses for the semester, wanting to end with grades that will reflect my level of commitment and make Captain proud. Afterward, I will concentrate my energies into this project that he, Baron, and I believe in so deeply. It's one thing to rescue someone from an unhealthy dynamic, but an abused submissive needs extra care and guidance. Not only to gain back her or his ability to trust again, but to also regain the joy that she or he once had as a submissive.

The fact that Baron and Captain not only care about these hurting submissives, but want to be actively involved in helping in their recovery, makes me so damn proud. I hope that, one day, Brie and Sir Davis will be able to join in our vision.

How amazing would that be?

Baron and I have been visiting local clubs to let the managers know about our program, so they can alert us if they come across subs in need. It feels good to be involved in something that will have a profound impact on lives now and in the future.

As I wait for Captain's return, I find myself drawn to visiting the Davises. After a long Saturday cleaning the last of the equipment in Baron's basement to ready it for our first official session, I make a special trip to visit Sir Davis and Brie at the hospital.

As soon as I walk into the room, an unexpected feeling of excitement surrounds me.

"Oh, Candy! We've *just* received the best news!" Brie cries as soon as she sees me.

I grab her hands and squeeze them tight. "Tell me! Tell me!"

"They've rescued Rytsar and everyone is accounted for, including dear Captain."

I throw my arms around her, crying, "Oh, thank God. That is the best news ever!"

"Not everyone came out unscathed, however," Sir Davis warns me. "Mr. Wallace is headed home to receive much-needed medical attention."

"What happened to him?" I ask Brie.

She is unable to speak as tears fall down her cheeks.

"He was tortured and lost an eye," Sir Davis answers for her.

"Oh, my God!" Although I'm not personal friends with the Dom, his blue eyes are legendary in the BDSM community. I can't stand that something happened to him, but the first thought that crosses my mind is: *Thank goodness Captain is there for him.*

"Was anyone else hurt?" I ask.

"Rytsar is in serious condition," Sir Davis informs me, his voice gruff with emotion. "Although Captain and Samantha were roughed up by their henchmen, they are both fine."

"When are they coming home?" I add hopefully, "Are they on their way now?"

Sir Davis shakes his head, a grave expression on his face. "Only Mr. Wallace is returning home at this point. The other three are planning to stay and eliminate the threat the Koslovs pose."

I feel my heart drop. "Why risk their lives when everyone made it out safely?"

Sir Davis looks at me with compassion. "I wish they were coming back now, as well, Miss Cox. However, the Koslovs are far more unstable than we thought. Captain and Rytsar agree they will continue to pose a threat to everyone who was involved in this rescue."

I look at Brie and whimper, "I'm not sure how much more of this I can take."

"I'm with you one hundred percent, Candy. I just want them to come home."

"They'll return immediately, once they complete this final task," Sir Davis assures me.

I can't lose Captain now...

"Miss Cox." Sir Davis motions me over to him.

I approach him slowly, my heart racing. I still find the ex-headmaster of the Submissive Training Center daunting, and knowing he has been through hell and back since the plane crash makes me feel even more so.

He holds out his hand to me, palm up on the bed. I tentatively place mine in his and instantly feel more at ease. When I lift my gaze and our eyes meet, I feel a profound connection to him and my fears begin to dissipate.

"I had a chance to speak to Captain briefly. He is already formulating a stratagem and is confident in their success. When I insisted he come home, he told me he could not leave in good conscience having witnessed the cruelty these men are capable of."

I nod, knowing that Captain would need to act after witnessing Faelan's torture. It's his nature, the way he's wired—and one of the reasons I love him.

"Like you, each second they remain in Russia eats at me. However, after speaking with Captain, I am convinced it is necessary." He leans forward to whisper in my ear. "He told me that you are what he fights for now."

My heart swells with pride, and it takes all my inner strength to hold back the tears. "I love that man."

"Your love is well placed."

When Sir Davis lets go of my hand, I feel fortified, as if he's passed some of his strength onto me. "Thank you."

I turn to Brie and hug her again. "Captain will see to

it they all come home."

"I'm glad we have each other while we wait," Brie confesses.

I look over at Sir Davis, taking a few moments before I speak, squeezing Brie's hand for courage. "I didn't want him to go, Sir Davis. But I knew he needed to for his own sake, as well as theirs."

"We're all grateful for his leadership."

"As much as I want him home with me, I know he has to finish what he's started there. No matter what happens, he's where he needs to be."

"You have a very mature perspective."

I smile sadly. "I've found—for me, at least—maturity doesn't come from age. It comes from grief. Once you accept it's a part of everyday life, it has less power to hold you hostage with fear."

"That is true, Miss Cox."

"However, that doesn't mean I'm not going to keep Captain all to myself when he gets back."

Sir Davis chuckles. "I'd say you've more than earned that time alone together."

I've been missing my parents and call them practically every day. I've told them Captain is away on an extended business trip, but they have no idea the danger he's in. It makes our conversations light, which is what I need right now.

"Would you consider coming to our house for the

holidays?" my mother asks.

Dad has informed me that Mom has had a few episodes recently, although they haven't lasted more than a couple of days. Still, I'm concerned and ask, "Are you sure you're up for the pressure, Mom?"

"I'm actually thinking having you two here is exactly what I need," she informs me.

I smile to myself, knowing she must already have a list of Christmas projects lined up for Captain.

"Hey, C," my dad says, "I've been rolling around an idea for a while and decided to act on it, but wanted to know your thoughts."

"Hit me, Dad."

"What if I told you that I talked to the high school about inviting Captain Walker to speak, and that they were enthusiastic about the idea? Do you think he would be interested in coming to his old alma mater and speaking to the students?"

"I'm not sure. He's a private man…but I personally think it's a fabulous idea. It would be good for him to see how respected he is in his hometown, and I know the students would gain valuable insight from what he'd have to share."

I'm excited at the prospect. Captain's family may have disowned him, but our town sure hasn't.

I'm suddenly hit with a flash of brilliance. "Of course, it's up to Charles whether he wants to return and speak at the high school but, if he says yes…"

I decide to share my idea with Dad.

It's almost a full three weeks before I get word that Captain is coming home!

He informs me while on the jet that not only was their final mission a success, but no one involved was hurt in the process. "We have nothing to fear now," he declares proudly.

I close my eyes, relief flowing through my veins. "I knew you would bring them all home safely."

"I'm coming home, just like I promised."

"I'll be waiting for you with bells on," I answer, crying happy tears.

Twelve hours later, the private jet rolls to a stop and the three of them emerge from the craft. For safety reasons, I'm not allowed to run out onto the tarmac to meet him, so I wait anxiously for Captain to turn and see me.

I'm jumping on the balls of my feet, the bell I've attached to my collar ringing as I squeak with excitement. The security guard takes pity on me and gives me a wink as he opens the gate.

I bolt toward Captain, running at full speed. Ms. Clark notices me first and nudges him. When Captain turns his head and sees me, he unceremoniously drops the bag in his hand and starts running to me.

I bound up and leap into his arms, wrapping my legs around him.

"Oh, my pet, my pet…"

I can't stop the happy tears as I pepper his face with

kisses before giving him a kiss on the lips. "My Captain has returned."

"How good it is to feel you in my arms," he says gruffly, kissing me more deeply.

The world disappears for a moment as we become lost in each other.

The fates have finally been kind.

Samantha comes up from behind, holding Captain's bag. "Don't let me interrupt, I just didn't want you to forget this." She nods to us and turns, her stilettos clicking against the concrete as she walks away.

Captain's gaze settles on my collar. "You have your bell on for me."

I open the lapel of the thin coat I'm wearing, revealing I have nothing else on underneath.

"Oh yes…" he growls seductively. "This is exactly what I have been imagining the entire time I've been gone."

"Take me home, Captain," I say, nuzzling his neck.

Still holding me, he picks up his bag. "Homeward bound, and we're not leaving it for a week."

"Or longer," I purr.

Captain doesn't even wait until we make it home. "I have needed you for too long, my pet," he growls.

Pulling into a closed business park, he drives around to the back and parks under the shade of a tree.

"Are you ready to be ravaged?"

My eyes widen, excited at the prospect of doing it right here and now. "Yes!"

Getting out of the car, he walks over to my door and opens it, commanding, "Then join me in the back."

I move to the back seat and he climbs in beside me. I giggle as he shuts the door and stares at me lustfully. "Let me see you wearing only my collar."

I glance around tentatively before untying my sash and unbuttoning my light coat. I open the thin material enough to expose my naked body to him.

The voracious look in his eye makes me weak with desire. Captain descends on me like a hungry cat, sucking, licking and even lightly biting. He pulls off my thin jacket and pushes me down onto the bench seat.

I close my eyes, moaning in ecstasy as he sucks on my breasts before nibbling on my neck.

"May I?" I ask breathlessly as I grab onto his belt.

"Yes, I have never wanted anyone as much as I want you," he growls huskily, plundering my mouth as I undo his belt and pants. He scoots me down farther, positioning his cock against my wet opening.

"Take me, Captain…" I beg.

He pushes his shaft slowly into me, making my pussy take the full length of him. We lay there for a moment, reveling in this intimate connection.

"Welcome home," I tell him, my heart bursting with my love for him.

"I love you, Candy," he declares as he begins thrusting.

My body molds to him as we make glorious love in his backseat, the bell ringing merrily while a bird chirps in the tree above us.

I have never felt so happy and alive.

Captain is home!

While Captain is off getting last-minute supplies with Baron for our first session in his dungeon, we get an unexpected phone call on the landline.

"Can I speak to Charles Walker?" a woman asks.

"I'm sorry. He's not here right now."

"This is urgent."

Something feels off, so I tell her, "I'll be sure to pass on your message to him."

"Are you his spouse?"

"Girlfriend," I reply curtly.

"I'm a nurse caring for Mr. Walker. He is dying and has requested his oldest son come to his bedside."

"Why does he want to see Charles now, after years of silence?"

"I cannot say."

I find it odd that it isn't Charles's mother or brother making such a call.

"Charles and his father are not on speaking terms," I inform her.

"I'm not familiar with their history, but Mr. Walker doesn't have much time left, Miss…?"

"My name is Miss Cox."

"Miss Cox, Mr. Walker has been asking for Charles for days now. He's quite insistent about wanting to talk to him."

I tremble, wondering if this will be the reconciliation Captain has been waiting for all of his adult life. "Let me write down your information. I'll be sure to pass it on when Captain Walker returns."

"Certainly." She gives me her contact information as well as the address of the VA hospital, stating afterward, "Miss Cox, Mr. Walker has dementia, but he has been cognizant the last few days and has been asking for his son constantly. Please let Charles Walker know that."

I start pacing the floor after I hang up. This could be an incredible opportunity to be reconciled with his father after all these years—but the man is dying.

I can barely contain myself when, hours later, he walks through the door. "Captain, I have news for you."

"What's wrong, pet?" he asks as soon as he sees my face.

"I received a call from a nurse…you may want to sit down."

Captain shakes his head, refusing to budge. "Tell me."

"I'm sorry, Captain, but your father is dying."

"I'm not sorry."

I shift nervously, unsure how he will react to the next bit of news. "He's been asking to see you."

"Did my mother call to tell you this?"

I shake my head. "No, it was a nurse who has been looking after him."

Captain frowns.

When he doesn't say anything, I add, "She told me he doesn't have much time left."

He sighs, wearing a tortured look when he tells me, "You have no idea how painful this is for me."

I wish I could take his pain away. "I'm so sorry."

Wrapping his powerful arms around me, Captain

says, "I've never told anyone what happened when Jacob and Mama came to visit me in the hospital after I returned to the States."

I have a feeling that what he is about to tell me will break my heart. "What happened, Captain?" I ask gently.

He says nothing, walking me over to the couch so we can sit down. Pulling me to him for comfort, I lay in his arms waiting for him to share his terrible secret.

Closure

Captain

I stare at Candy, hesitant to talk about the moment that left a scar on my soul for all of these years, but I trust her enough to expose the deepest wounds I carry.

"This must stay between us, pet."

"Of course, Captain. I would never betray your confidence."

I feel my stomach twist, thinking back on that meeting with the two people who were dearest to me. All those years in the service, and I had counted on reconciliation with my mother and brother.

Despite their silence, I believed that day would come, and I was right. But, it was nothing like I imagined...

It takes me a few minutes to compartmentalize my emotions before I let the events slowly unfold in my mind.

The extensive damage caused to the right side of my face by the explosion makes it feel as if my entire head is on fire. My brain cannot localize the pain, and I am completely consumed by it.

There is no reality other than Pain.

I long for escape, and I beg God for it.

If you are truly merciful, I beseech you to end this and let me die. Let me join my men…

But, I've known since I was young that God doesn't often give you what you ask for.

"Charles."

The voice is so familiar and dear, I actually stop breathing for a moment.

"Oh, Charles…" Her voice breaks and she begins to sob. The sound of my mother crying pulls at my heart.

I turn my head toward her and open my one good eye. It takes a few moments for my eye to adjust as her outline comes into focus. I see my mother standing beside the bed, along with a young man dressed in an Air Force uniform.

It must be Jacob, but the expression on his face makes my blood run cold. I see nothing but disgust and anger in his eyes—and it is eerily reminiscent of my father.

My mother's sobs rip at my heart and I lift my hand to her, forgetting my own pain.

"Don't cry, Mama."

She shakes her head, crying even more. "Look what's happened to my little boy…"

I swallow hard.

I've missed her so much that my heart aches. "I love

you, Mama."

She whimpers, tears streaming down her face, but she's unable to look at me. "Charles, why did you have to choose this life? You didn't have to end up this way."

Her words hit me hard in the chest. My injuries are not something I *chose*, and I stare at her in disbelief.

Jacob growls, "Haven't you caused our family enough torment?"

I turn my gaze to him. I don't recognize the cold-hearted man standing before me. The brother I knew no longer exists. "I don't know what's happened to you, Jacob."

"What happened is that you ran away from your duty to your family like a coward, leaving me to pick up the pieces."

"That's not what happened."

"Don't try to rewrite history now that you are helpless and alone. You made your choice, choosing the Army over family, and I can never forgive you for it."

It's like listening to my father all over again and I grimace in pain. My blood pressure is rising, making my entire head pound in agony.

Jacob stares down at me accusingly. "You abandoned us, Charlie, and never once looked back. Do you know how many nights Mama has cried herself to sleep? Do you?"

"What about the letters? I wrote you every damn Tuesday for years without one fucking response from you."

"Liar!" he spits. "You would say anything to get back in our good graces now that you have no one to take care of you."

I look to my mother. She knows the truth. "What happened to all the letters?"

"I never saw any letters—except one. A young woman handed it to me in the grocery store, claiming it was from you. She claimed a lot of things…"

"What did you do with the letter, Mama?"

"I gave it to your father, unopened. I didn't have a choice. Those were my orders if I ever received anything from you."

"Why would you do that?" I cry in disbelief.

"You know your father. If I had opened that letter, he would have seen it as a betrayal. I couldn't risk losing Jacob, too…"

I glance back at my little brother. "I never stopped thinking about you, Jacob. It's not my fault Father erased me from your life."

His stare is cold and unsympathetic. "You didn't have to leave us."

"I did."

"And look where it's gotten you," he says, laughing sarcastically.

I growl under my breath, refusing to listen to my father speaking to me through my brother. "Why have you come?" I demand.

"To let you know we are aware of your situation and will not be helping you. You created this situation, and now you must live with it."

I stare at him, unable to reconcile the boy I once knew with the man standing before me now, and feel a sense of regret. "I'm sorry I wasn't there to save you."

Jacob frowns. "I don't need saving, you pompous ass."

"You're right. It's too late."

He shakes his head in disgust. "I can't believe I ever looked up to you." Turning to my mother, he snarls, "It's time to go. We did what we came here for."

Jacob walks off, not bothering to look back.

My mother still cannot bear to look at me and fumbles through her purse, pulling out a large wad of cash. "This is money I've been saving a little at a time over the years so your father wouldn't notice." She stuffs the money in my hand. "I want you to have all of it."

I don't want the money—I only want her to stay. "Don't go, Mama."

She braves a quick glance at me. "I love you, Charles…"

"Mama," Jacob barks sternly from the doorway.

"Goodbye," she whispers.

My throat constricts as I watch her hurry to join Jacob.

I have never felt so utterly alone.

"I can't even imagine," Candy says when I finish, tears running down her face. Wrapping her arms around me, she lays her head on my chest. "I'm so sorry they did that to you…"

I gladly accept her hug. I've suffered too long with the memory to show any outward emotion, but it still hurts deeply.

"Did they ever reconcile with you?" she asks.

"No. I never saw them again."

She looks up at me. "How could your brother be so cruel to you?"

"He was parroting what my father told him. I'm convinced Jacob was brainwashed." Tears come to my eye. "He was a sweet kid once. I hate that my father took that from him."

"But why would your mother go along with it?"

"With time, I've come to understand. I believe when I left to join the Army, she had to make a choice. It was either Jacob or me, and he was just a little boy. Had she taken a stand against my father, I guarantee he would have cut her out, as well. The fact is…Jacob needed her more than I did, so she stayed."

"But she didn't even open your letter."

"I've thought about that as well and realized she couldn't take that chance. Ellen gave it to my mother in a public place, which was the worst thing she could have done. My father is a control freak, and people in small towns talk. My mother couldn't risk hiding the letter from him in case someone mentioned it to him." I sigh deeply. "And because of that, Jacob was never given the chance to decide his own fate."

Candy smiles sadly. "You still love your brother, don't you?"

"I don't care for the person he's become, but I remember the boy he once was, and I loved him dearly. I have to believe that part of him still exists."

"I don't understand your father."

"I don't, either, but I've stopped caring at this point."

She lays her head on my chest. "I wish I could make up for all he's done."

I wrap my arms around her, squeezing her tight. "You have, my pet. Don't you know my world has changed because you're in it?"

We sit there for several minutes before she asks the question that has been burning in my heart ever since I got the news. "What if your father is sorry for what he's done?"

"Why should I give him the satisfaction of a peaceful death when I have suffered every day since he cut me out of their lives? How is that fair?"

"That's a valid point, but…if he's sincere, it might finally bring you some closure. At the very least, you would have a chance to confront him."

I sit there, contemplating what to do. On one hand, the thought of him dying without having the final word has a great appeal. At the same time, if there is a chance of closure, it might be worth the risk it poses to my soul.

Might…

To Candy's credit, she does not try to persuade me one way or the other, understanding that this is a very personal decision.

Do I err on the side of justice and let him suffer his last moments, or do I risk being hurt again in the hopes that he will admit he was wrong?

I book plane tickets for us the next day deciding— today, at least—to be an optimist.

Candy takes my hand as we board the plane. It is her

strength I lean on during that long plane ride. My only consolation in going to see my father is that he was moved to a hospital in another state.

I am grateful not to have to face my hometown, on top of confronting my father.

I walk into the hospital room behind the nurse. My muscles are tense—ready for battle.

I'm extremely grateful to have Candy beside me. No matter how this plays out, I know she will stand by me.

Seeing my father lying in the hospital bed, he seems so much smaller than I remember. It's a jolt to my system to think this wrinkled, gray-haired man is the same person, but it's been more than thirty years since we had that confrontation at the house.

Still, even knowing that, I'm shocked by how severely his body has been ravaged by time.

The man stares blankly ahead at nothing, unaware that we are there.

The nurse goes up to the bed to speak with him. "Look who came to visit you today, Mr. Walker. It's your son, Charles. The one you have been asking for."

His brows furrow, and he turns his head slightly to her. "Who?"

"Your oldest son, Charles."

She waves me to come closer.

I hesitate for a moment, before walking up to the bed.

"Father."

He continues to stare at the nurse, as if he hasn't heard me.

"Sometimes it takes him a while to respond to people," she explains. "Just keep talking to him."

The nurse smiles at me and nods to Candy before leaving us alone with him.

I look down at him, shocked that this shriveled old man was once my father. I actually feel pity for him.

"Mr. Walker," Candy says, moving to the other side of the bed and leaning in close. "Your son came to see you. He's right here."

He slowly turns his gaze on her. "Who are you?"

She glances at me and smiles. "I'm your son's girl-friend."

"My son?"

"Yes. Charles, standing beside you," she says, pointing to me.

Father turns his head toward me and frowns. "You're not my son."

Despite my age, his words still have the power to cut me like a knife.

"Yes, this is your oldest son, Charles," Candy repeats. "He's traveled a long way to see you."

My father shakes his head, looking away from me. "My first son died. That's not him."

"It is me, Father," I say in a stern voice. "I'm most definitely *not* dead."

"No," he insists, looking at Candy when he says, "Charles died when he was eighteen."

I can't tell if he is deliberately trying to bait me or if,

in his dementia, he truly believes I'm dead.

Candy dutifully corrects him. "Charles has come today to see you because you said you had something you wanted to say to him."

His expression becomes ugly and he yells at her. "He's dead! I can't talk to a dead man."

I look at Candy apologetically. She should not have to tolerate him yelling at her whether he has dementia or not.

Realizing it's pointless to argue with Father about who I am, I ask instead, "What do you remember about Charles?"

He gazes up at the ceiling, licking his lips absently as if he hasn't heard me.

I look over at Candy, ready to leave.

However, Candy isn't ready to give up quite yet. Taking his shriveled hand in hers, she asks him, "Mr. Walker, what did you want to tell your son Charles?"

For several moments, he stares down at her hand holding his. "I…"

I wait, wondering if his answer will be affirming, or simply one more nail in the coffin of my hatred for him.

Why the hell did I come?

"I had two sons."

"Yes…" Candy says, encouraging him to continue.

"But a father always has his favorite."

I turn away, disgusted I've traveled all this way to hear this.

"Charles was mine."

His words strike at my heart. I do not feel vindicated by his confession—I am angry.

I turn back to face him. "How *dare* you say that! You disowned me, keeping me from my family all these years, and *now* you want to claim I was your favorite? Did Jacob mean nothing to you?"

I grab the rail of his bed and shake it. "Damn you, Father. You manipulated that poor kid with your malicious lies. I feel nothing but disgust for you and everything you have done to this family."

I hold out my hand to Candy. "There's no reason to remain here any longer."

She takes my hand, but looks clearly distressed as we walk out the door.

"Charles…"

I stop, because the tone in his voice has changed. It sounds as if he's speaking to me directly, so I turn around.

I can tell by the clarity of his gaze that he is lucid— briefly breaking through the fog of his dementia.

I step back into the room with Candy beside me. "Father?"

He stares at me for several seconds, his eyes unblinking. "You were my greatest disappointment."

I squeeze Candy's hand.

Taking a few moments to collect my thoughts, I respond. "I've strived my entire life to be nothing like you, so I'm glad I've disappointed you, *sir*."

"You always were an arrogant boy," he snarls.

I smile as I put my arm around Candy. "I have the love of a beautiful woman, a group of friends I consider family, and a vocation I believe in. I've done exceedingly well without your approval and I certainly don't need it now."

I turn around and escort Candy out of the room. For the briefest of moments, I am tempted to return to his bedside and condemn him for every wrong he has committed, but the man dying in that bed is lonely and bitter—and that is enough for me.

I leave the hospital grateful that I came.

"Are you okay?" Candy asks pensively as the two of us walk to the car.

"I am, my pet," I answer, smiling at her. "Seeing him again has given me closure."

Her lip trembles. "I'm so sorry for the terrible things he said to you."

I snort. "It's nothing I haven't heard before—except for that crap about being his favorite. Whether or not it's true, I don't want that ever repeated. Jacob's suffered enough under that man."

"I won't ever mention it," Candy promises.

I look back at the hospital, knowing I will never see my father alive again—and I am fine with that.

After all these years, he no longer holds any power over me.

Tribute

Candy

Ever since that meeting with his father, I have struggled to think about anything else. The idea that the man responsible for Captain's life and upbringing could be so cruel, even on his deathbed, tears at my heart.

Captain tells me he's fine, and I believe him, but he deserves so much more, and my parents and I have been working on a plan to give him exactly that.

It begins with a letter:

```
Dear Captain Walker,
Sub: INVITATION TO SPEAK AT RILEY HIGH
SCHOOL

The entire staff of Riley High School
would be honored if you would speak to
our students on November 17 at 10 a.m.
in the school auditorium. We are asking
a number of former graduates to share
their personal experiences and the
```

```
lessons they have learned outside of
school.
    We hope to inspire the up and coming
leaders represented in our student body
through those who have graduated from
Riley and gone on to distinguish
themselves.
With warm regards,
Katharine Walsh
Principal
Riley High School
```

Captain actually laughs after reading the letter. "Can you believe this? The new principal at Riley High wants *me* to speak at an assembly." He tosses it on the counter dismissively.

I stare at it, knowing how important it is.

"I'm not surprised, actually," I tell him. "My dad was telling me that they plan to knock down the old school and are already breaking ground on the new one."

"Knock down Riley High?" Captain picks up the letter again. "So this is like a last hurrah for the old school?"

"Something like that."

He looks at me. "Sad to think our school will cease to exist."

"I know… A lot of memories are tied up in that place."

"Well…" He reads the letter again. "I might consider it, despite all the bad history I have with that town." He glances at me. "See if your parents are open to us paying them a visit."

"Are you serious?" I squeak.

He smiles at me tenderly. "You're too cute, my pet. That reaction right there just solidified my decision to go."

"Do you mind if I call to ask my parents right now?"

"Go right ahead." He glances at the letter again. "Damn…now I have to figure out what the hell I'm going to say to all those kids."

I giggle as I pick up the phone.

Everything is going according to plan.

Captain, Baron and I are busy every night running our second session with submissives. Although our program is based on some of the same principals as the Submissive Training Center, our curriculum moves at a much slower pace and focuses more on the emotional aspect of the power exchange rather than the mechanics.

We want each of our charges to grow in their understanding of the essential characteristics of a healthy BDSM partnership on a personal level, and then build on their experience from there. It isn't as cut and dry as the curriculum at the Center, but the breakthroughs we have already witnessed have been truly inspiring. It's what we live for now.

Our busy schedule means that Captain has no time to reflect on his upcoming speech or give much thought about what he is going to say.

When the day arrives to fly out, he is caught off

guard.

"Candy, I hate to disappoint you, but we're going to have to cancel."

"What are you talking about?"

"I haven't written my speech. The last thing they want is a one-eyed freak on stage babbling like an idiot."

"Don't ever talk about my Master that way again," I scold him.

He winks at me, but replies, "I'm serious. I've got nothing."

I wrap my arms around him and rub my cheek against him. "We'll figure it out on the plane ride there. It doesn't have to be anything fancy."

"True...they did say other people are coming."

I blush slightly and am glad he doesn't notice. "Why don't you wear your uniform?"

"Why would I do that?"

"I heard the principal has something planned for the people arriving today."

"It seems totally unnecessary to me."

I bat my eyes at him. "You know how crazy it makes me when you wear your uniform, Captain."

With a bit of prodding, I convince him to wear the uniform *and* get on the plane with me. On the flight there, I ask him about the struggles he had getting his college degree while serving in the Army, as well as what it took for him to survive the wounds he suffered in battle and how that changed him.

After listening to him, I'm all choked up. "Captain, if you share any of that, I'm sure you'll give students who are struggling right now the encouragement they need to keep fighting."

He nods thoughtfully. "If I can help even one see beyond the scars they carry—internal or external—that would make any humiliation I face on stage worth it."

"That's the spirit!" I tell him.

Once we land, we're greeted by a young man in an Army uniform holding up a sign that reads *Captain Walker*.

Captain looks at me. "What's that about?"

I shrug, struggling to keep from smiling.

The man holds out his hand when Captain walks up.

"Captain Walker, it is an honor to meet you, sir. I joined the Army because of you."

"Because of me?"

"Yes, sir. I passed your photo every day in the hallway at Riley High. You inspired me to serve. I'm on my second tour of duty."

Captain shakes his hand again, patting him on the arm with the other hand. "It's a sincere pleasure to meet you."

"Thank you, sir." He glances at me and smiles. "I've come to drive you both to your hotel."

"You don't need to do that..." Captain glances at the name on his uniform, "...Second Lieutenant Martin."

"I insist, and I'll get your bags, as well."

Captain raises an eyebrow, but acquiesces. Wrapping an arm around me, we follow the young Lieutenant to the baggage claim, and then to his car.

The red car Lieutenant Martin leads us to gets a whistle from Captain. "Wow, a 1976 Cadillac Eldorado convertible. You don't see those every day."

"No, you don't, sir." He sounds proud when he opens the door for us, and puts our luggage in the back. "I assume you want the top down?" he asks Captain.

"By all means."

Captain grins as we pull out of the garage and start down the road. "I never dreamed in a million years I'd be coming back in something as stylish as this."

He puts his arm around me, his expression carefree like that of a teenager. It makes my heart flutter just looking at him.

Captain points to a small group of people standing on the side of the road, holding signs. "Would you look at that," he says, pointing them out to me.

As we pass, they start waving and cheering. Captain's smile freezes as he reads their homemade signs.

Welcome Home, Captain Walker!

You are my hero!

Army Proud

He turns his head as we pass by them and waves robotically, still in shock.

We pass another group who are more vocal and have noisemakers.

"What is this?" he asks me.

"They've all come out to welcome you home, Captain," I tell him.

Captain looks at me as if he can't quite process what is happening. Meanwhile, another group cheers him on from the roadside. He waves at them, still shaking his head.

With each passing group, he begins waving more enthusiastically, reading each sign out loud as tears run down his scarred cheek. "The whole town's come out…" he says in awe.

I have never been happier or more moved than I am at this moment as I watch Captain receiving the proper homecoming he deserves.

When we arrive at the hotel, my parents are waiting for us with signs of their own. Captain just shakes his head, trying to hold in the emotions as Lieutenant Martin opens the car door for us.

"Thank you for this incredible ride, Second Lieutenant Martin," he manages to say, his voice raw with emotion.

"It has been my sincere pleasure, Captain Walker."

Captain then turns to my parents. "Something tells me you had something to do with this."

My father's huge grin answers the question before Captain even speaks. "We felt it was high time you were given the honor you deserve in your hometown."

Captain just keeps shaking his head. "I have no words."

"None are needed," my mother replies. "Welcome home, Captain Walker."

He gives her a hug, holding it longer than normal. My mom smiles at me, loving every second of it.

When we finally lay down to sleep at the end of the night, Captain tells me, "I don't think anything will ever top today." He turns his head toward me. "Thank you,

Candy."

I'm smiling so hard it hurts. "I love you, Captain."

"Sweet pet, this man loves you more than words can say."

I fall asleep in his arms, knowing that what's coming tomorrow will totally blow him away...

The next morning, Captain dresses in his uniform once more. "This is the first time in—I can't tell you how many years—that I've worn this uniform two days in a row."

I purr, "Well, you know *I'm* not complaining."

We arrive at the high school an hour early at the principal's request.

"Captain Walker, I'm Principal Katharine Walsh. Can I just say how pleased I was to hear that you agreed to speak with our students today?"

He takes her hand to shake it, cocking his head as he chuckles. "I can't promise the kids will stay awake for my portion, but I'll do my best."

"I've heard from several people that you have a quick wit."

Captain throws back his head and laughs. "I'm sorry, Principal Walsh, but someone has been feeding you a load of horsesh—"

A young woman hurries past, sporting a backpack.

Captain instantly closes his mouth. After she disappears into one of the nearby classrooms, he lets his breath out. "And that is why you don't invite people like me into educational institutions."

Principal Walsh laughs. "I'm not worried in the least, Captain Walker. Why don't I show you around the school while we wait?"

My, it feels weird walking the halls of Riley High again, and I can't begin to imagine how strange it must be for Captain after so many years away. For me, there are ghosts of Ethan still haunting these halls, but instead of sadness, I feel a sense of connection with him.

There is real comfort in seeing that our high school has pretty much stayed the same, including the trophy case with Captain's picture in it.

"See?" I say, pointing excitedly at the display case devoted just to him.

Captain shakes his head as he stares at his high school track picture. "I've forgotten that I was ever that young."

I gush, "I had a secret crush on you. Even though you look dashing in that track uniform, it's the Army one I fell in love with."

Captain stares at the photo. I can tell by the stoic expression on his face, he is going through a myriad of emotions but trying desperately to hide it.

"You'll be happy to know that the display case is going to the new school after it's built," Principal Walsh informs us.

"Would it be okay if I added something to it?" he asks her.

"Certainly. Let me go get the keys."

As she hurries off, Captain pulls out his wallet and takes out his picture of Grapes. He looks at it fondly. "He deserves to be honored, too."

When the principal returns, he shows the picture to her. "This was my Battle Buddy in boot camp. His name was Adam Bell, but we all knew him as Grapes." Captain holds out his wrist, showing her his tattoo. "He went on to become an officer and died bravely for this country." Captain looks her in the eye when he adds, "He also happened to be my best friend."

"We'll be sure to add a small plaque with his name to the display."

"That would mean a lot to me," Captain tells her, tucking Grapes photo beside his own when she opens the case.

Afterward, he stands back and smiles. "Look at that. Grapes and BS…together again."

Students start filing out of their classrooms as they head for the auditorium.

Ms. Walsh quickly directs us to the stage area. "Miss Cox, we have a chair reserved for you next to your parents. Feel free to take a seat when you're ready."

"Thank you, Ms. Walsh. For everything," I tell her, knowing the incredible amount of effort she has put into this event.

"My pleasure," she answers warmly.

Principal Walsh turns to Captain. "Captain Walker, please wait here until I make your introduction."

"I won't move from the spot until you do," he assures her.

Captain watches her walk off and then turns to me, sighing anxiously. "How is it that an old war veteran can feel this nervous over a simple speech?"

"You have nothing to worry about, Captain," I say confidently. "Today is all about you. Enjoy it."

I give him a kiss on the cheek and wish him luck before scooting down the stairs of the stage to sit with my family.

As I go to sit down, my dad asks, "Do you think he knows?"

I grin. "Nope, he has no idea."

Full Circle

Captain

I wait in the wings, feeling like a fool as I rub my ice-cold hands together. There's no reason I should be apprehensive about speaking to an auditorium full of teenagers—but I am.

When Principal Walsh calls my name, I hear an overly enthusiastic round of applause that seems odd given the circumstances. I walk out onto the stage with forced confidence, looking out over the sea of students sitting in the theater seats.

I remember sitting in those seats and I nod to the students before heading toward the podium. I notice a number of people sitting in chairs on the stage. With so many speaking today, it takes the pressure off my own speech and I relax a little.

"Captain Walker, I'm afraid I haven't been completely honest about why you're here today," Principal Walsh informs me.

I look at her in confusion as the lights go dim and

the entire auditorium becomes eerily silent. Up on the screen, a video starts playing.

I'm shocked to see footage of myself at the high school track back when I was only seventeen. For the next fifteen minutes, I watch the major events of my life play out on the screen. There's even a segment highlighting both Trouper and Echo.

Afterward, the lights come back up and I'm left standing there, speechless.

"Captain Walker, you might be wondering who these other people are," she says, pointing to those on the stage. "They're from this school and have come here today to tell you in person about the significant difference you've made in their lives."

I look at the group of strangers in stunned silence, then scan the auditorium for Candy. She's sitting in the front row with her parents, wearing a huge smile on her face.

A man close to my age, gets up first and walks over to me.

"Captain Walker, I was a sophomore your senior year in high school, so you wouldn't remember me, but your excellence in track and field was a true inspiration. I studied your techniques and went on to compete on the national level, finally making the Olympic Team in 1980."

I hold out my hand to shake his, profoundly impressed to meet an Olympian, from Riley High no less. "What an honor it is to meet you."

"The honor is mine, Captain Walker. Your determination became my inspiration." He points to the others sitting there. "It was to many of us."

One after another, they come up to share their story—the amputee skier encouraged by Captain's single-minded, no excuses attitude, to the surgeon who was inspired to follow her calling and is now recognized for a breakthrough procedure in her field.

I'm awestruck by each of these accomplished individuals. It's humbling that they credit me for influencing them and I struggle to keep my emotions in check.

"Captain Walker, there is one more person who has come here to see you today." Principal Walsh leaves the stage for a moment, then comes back a few moments later helping a bent, old man in his eighties onto the stage.

I stare at him for a second before recognizing the man. "Mr. Hall!" I cry out, running across the stage to him. "I can't believe you're here!"

Mr. Hall looks up at me, his eyes sparkling. "What an honor it is to see you again, Captain Walker. I always knew you would do great things."

I turn to the students, declaring, "You can't know the difference this man made at a crucial time in my life. He gave me a word of encouragement, a meal, and even saw me off the next day as I headed out to meet my destiny." I turn back to him, putting my hand over my heart. "Thank you, Mr. Hall."

He chuckles. "No, thank you. You have been an inspiration to me all these years, young man."

I laugh at being called young and hug him again. I realize I've lost so much by leaving this place behind—and this man standing before me is one of them. To be given this chance to thank him personally is a rare gift.

I nod my thanks to Principal Walsh, then turn to Candy and mouth the words, *Thank you*.

My time has finally come to speak. I stand at the podium, looking over this group of young people, impressed by their level of energy and limitless potential.

"You've probably heard enough about me to last you a lifetime, so I'll keep this brief. It's all well and good for people to spout platitudes and affirmations. Nothing wrong with that.

"However, that's not my style—never has been. I'm a free-thinker, and there have been times when it's gotten me in trouble."

I scan the crowd and my eyes are drawn to two people standing in the back of the auditorium. For a moment, my mouth goes dry.

My gaze darts to Candy, wondering if this is yet another surprise she has planned. She turns to look back to where I'm staring and spots the two. Turning back to me, she shrugs, appearing not to know them.

The silence in the auditorium drags on for too long and I hear uncomfortable chatter from the audience. I clear my throat, trying to regain my composure even though my mind is racing, trying to figure out why Jacob and my mother have come.

Not one to mince words, I continue with my speech as planned. "I've lost some very important people in my life, been crippled and forgotten, but I've kept on fighting each day because I had discovered a simple but valuable truth early on in my life. This is what I want you to walk away with today, so listen carefully…"

I pause for a moment, making sure I have everyone's attention—including my brother's.

"Your soul will never be quiet until you fulfill your destiny."

I smile encouragingly at all those youthful faces staring up at me. "If you understand that, life becomes a whole lot simpler. I'm not saying it will be easy...just look at me." There is good-natured chuckling in the crowd. "However, I followed my destiny starting at the age you are right now, and I've never veered from it. I can tell you from experience, it was the best decision I ever made.

"The life I lead now is based on choices I made along the way. Circumstances may sway your path momentarily, but you ultimately decide the direction you take."

I stare at my mother and brother when I say, "I have no regrets. I followed my destiny, and I wish the same for all of you."

I turn to Principal Walsh to shake her hand. "Thank you for orchestrating all of this."

She smiles, wiping away a tear. "What you shared with our students will reverberate for generations to come, I'm sure. Thank you, Captain Walker."

I head down the steps to join Candy, and we are immediately surrounded by students as they come up wanting to talk to me. I look up briefly to see that my family is gone.

I'm not surprised and refuse to dwell on it, choosing instead to invest my time and attention on the future leaders of Riley High.

Two hours later, we finally make it out of the school, and head toward the car. I stop short when I see Jacob and my mother waiting for me in the parking lot.

I put my arm around Candy protectively as we approach them. I immediately notice that my mother's eyes are red and her cheeks tearstained as if she has been crying the entire time.

"Why are you here?" I demand of my brother.

"I don't know if you heard, but Father died last week."

"I knew he was dying, but not that he had finally passed," I reply, offering nothing more.

My mother speaks up. "We've been cleaning out the house. I don't live there anymore."

"And what does that have to do with me?" I ask tersely, turning back to Jacob.

"This..." he answers, opening the back of a hatchback parked next to them.

Inside is a large plastic box. He lifts the lid, and pulls out a letter.

I stared at it in disbelief. "My letters...?"

"Father kept them hidden in the attic."

That fucking bastard! I think to myself. Because I was his "favorite" he couldn't bear to throw my letters away, but he never let Jacob read a single one.

"They're all here," he continues, "in chronological order." Jacob's voice is strained when he tells me, "Father never opened them, but Mama and I read through them all within the last twenty-four hours."

Mama sobs, "Charles…"

I can't handle her pain, but I remain rooted where I am beside Candy. I've been hurt too many times by my family not to be cautious now.

"Charlie, I'm sorry I didn't believe you," Jacob tells me, barely able to look me in the eye.

"Father was an expert manipulator," I reply curtly.

Jacob winces. "When I think how I spoke to you that day at the hospital…"

I only shake my head, the pain of that visit still raw like a fresh wound.

"My boy, how we've wronged you," my mother cries.

Oh, to finally hear those words come from one of my own. I walk over to my mother, wrapping my arms around her. "I forgive you, Mama…I know that what you did, you did to protect Jacob."

She starts sobbing uncontrollably. Candy opens her purse and pulls out a wad of tissues for me. I hand one to my mother, murmuring gently, "It's okay, Mama…"

Jacob takes the letter out of the envelope in his hand, and begins reading.

"Dear Jacob, I know things were pretty messed up when I left, but don't worry about me. I'm okay. Great, in fact. But now that you're second in command, I need to ask a favor, little man. Can you look after Mom? Pitch in when she needs help and give her an extra hug from me from time to time. As for Father, he deserves your respect. He's done a good job preparing us for military life, and I'm grateful for his training despite the huge fight we had. As far as that's concerned, I hope what you take away from it is how vitally important it is to be true to yourself, no matter what. I have no regrets…"

His voice falters and he can't finish.

"That was the very first letter I wrote," I tell him.

He nods, running his hand over the rows and rows of letters in the box. "You wrote me every Tuesday, just like you said." His eyes start tearing up. "I'm sorry, big brother…"

I see in those sad eyes the little boy I once knew and instinctively hold my arms out to him. "Little man."

Jacob moves forward and throws his arms around me, slapping me hard on the back. "I've missed you, Charlie."

I stiffen. It takes me a moment to realize that he's lived our relationship in the span of a day through the letter I've written, while I still carry years of heartache and resentment caused by his banishment.

I have a choice.

I can hold onto those feelings and continue to nurse them, or I can forgive Jacob and embrace this gift I've been given.

"I love you, Jacob. I always have."

A feeling of unity washes over me in that moment. In reconnecting with my family, I feel the collective joy of all those who have gone before me—from Grapes, my men, and even the pups.

I've touched that elusive truth Candy discovered that night with Nosaka, and I am finally able to let the guilt of surviving that horrific day go after all these years. I turn to Candy and hold out my arms to her, needing her to be a part of this profound moment.

Looking up at the sky with my brother and mother by my side, and my beautiful woman in my arms, I let out a long, loud cry of victory.

I hope you enjoyed ***Destined to Dominate!***

Coming next is—***Sir's Rise: Rise of the Dominants Book One***, the first of a trilogy.

Find out how a man becomes a Master.

Thane Davis is a young man without a father and a manipulative mother he wants to escape from.

In an attempt to reclaim his life, he advances his studies, determined to succeed in the business world.

New friends will become lifelong brothers and in the process, Thane will be educated in the seductive world of Domination…

(Release Date – November 6th, 2018)

Or, if you are new to Brie and the gang, you can begin the journey with the 1st Box Set of ***Brie's Submission*** which is FREE!

COMING NEXT

Sir's Rise:
Rise of the Dominants Book One
Available for Preorder

Reviews mean the world to me!

I truly appreciate you taking the time to review ***Destined to Dominate***.

If you could leave a review on both Goodreads and the site where you purchased this eBook from, I would be so grateful. Sincerely, ~Red

Don't miss the background stories behind the characters you read about in ***Safe Haven & Destined to Dominate.***

You can begin the journey with the 1st Box Set of *Brie's Submission* which is FREE!

1-Click here for your FREE box set
And start reading NOW!

ABOUT THE AUTHOR

Over Two Million readers have enjoyed Red's stories

Red Phoenix – USA Today Bestselling Author
Winner of 8 Readers' Choice Awards

Hey Everyone!

I'm Red Phoenix, an author who also happens to be a submissive in real life. I wrote the Brie's Submission series because I wanted people everywhere to know just how much fun BDSM can be.

There is a huge cast of characters who are part of Brie's journey. The further you read into the story the more you learn about each one. I hope you grow to love Brie and the gang as much as I do.

They've become like family.

When I'm not writing, you can find me online with readers.

I heart my fans! ~Red

To find out more visit my Website

redphoenixauthor.com

Follow Me on BookBub

bookbub.com/authors/red-phoenix

Newsletter: Sign up

redphoenixauthor.com/newsletter-signup

Facebook: RedPhoenix69

Twitter: @redphoenix69

Instagram: RedPhoenixAuthor

I invite you to join my reader Group!

facebook.com/groups/539875076052037

SIGN UP FOR MY NEWSLETTER
HERE FOR THE LATEST RED
PHOENIX UPDATES

SALES, GIVEAWAYS, NEW
RELEASES, EXCLUSIVE SNEAK
PEEKS, AND MORE!
SIGN UP HERE
REDPHOENIXAUTHOR.COM/NEWSLETTER-
SIGNUP

Red Phoenix is the author of:

Brie's Submission Series:

Teach Me #1

Love Me #2

Catch Me #3

Try Me #4

Protect Me #5

Hold Me #6

Surprise Me #7

Trust Me #8

Claim Me #9

Enchant Me #10

A Cowboy's Heart #11

Breathe with Me #12

Her Russian Knight #13

Under His Protection #14

Her Russian Returns #15

In Sir's Arms #16

Bound by Love #17

*You can also purchase the AUDIO BOOK **Versions**

Also part of the Submissive Training Center world:

Captain's Duet

Safe Haven

Destined to Dominate

Rise of the Dominates Trilogy

Sir's Rise #1

Book Two Coming Spring '19

Book Three Coming Summer '19

Other Books by Red Phoenix

Blissfully Undone
* Available in eBook and paperback

(Snowy Fun—Two people find themselves snowbound in a cabin where hidden love can flourish, taking one couple on a sensual journey into ménage à trois)

His Scottish Pet: Dom of the Ages
* Available in eBook and paperback

Audio Book: *His Scottish Pet: Dom of the Ages*

(Scottish Dom—A sexy Dom escapes to Scotland in the late 1400s. He encounters a waif who has the potential to free him from his tragic curse)

The Erotic Love Story of Amy and Troy
* Available in eBook and paperback

(Sexual Adventures—True love reigns, but fate continually throws Troy and Amy into the arms of others)

eBooks

Varick: The Reckoning

(Savory Vampire—A dark, sexy vampire story. The hero navigates the dangerous world he has been thrust into with lusty passion and a pure heart)

Keeper of the Wolf Clan (Keeper of Wolves, #1)

(Sexual Secrets—A virginal werewolf must act as the clan's mysterious Keeper)

The Keeper Finds Her Mate (Keeper of Wolves, #2)

(Second Chances—A young she-wolf must choose between old ties or new beginnings)

The Keeper Unites the Alphas (Keeper of Wolves, #3)

(Serious Consequences—The young she-wolf is captured by the rival clan)

Boxed Set: Keeper of Wolves Series (Books 1-3)

(Surprising Secrets—A secret so shocking it will rock Layla's world. The young she-wolf is put in a position of being able to save her werewolf clan or becoming the reason for its destruction)

Socrates Inspires Cherry to Blossom

(Satisfying Surrender—A mature and curvaceous woman becomes fascinated by an online Dom who has much to teach her)

By the Light of the Scottish Moon

(Saving Love—Two lost souls, the Moon, a werewolf, and a death wish…)

In 9 Days

(Sweet Romance—A young girl falls in love with the new student, nicknamed "the Freak")

---

9 Days and Counting

(Sacrificial Love—The sequel to *In 9 Days* delves into the emotional reunion of two longtime lovers)

And Then He Saved Me

(Saving Tenderness—When a young girl tries to kill herself, a man of great character intervenes with a love that heals)

Play With Me at Noon

(Seeking Fulfillment—A desperate wife lives out her
fantasies by taking five different men in five days)

Connect with Red on Substance B

Substance B is a platform for independent authors to directly connect with their readers. Please visit Red's Substance B page where you can:

- Sign up for Red's newsletter
- Send a message to Red
- See all platforms where Red's books are sold

Visit Substance B today to learn more about your favorite independent authors.

Made in the USA
Columbia, SC
19 July 2020